LEAVING
MILAN

ALSO BY ELIZABETH ONESS

Articles of Faith

Departures

Twelve Rivers of the Body

Fallibility

LEAVING

MILAN

BY
ELIZABETH ONESS

BRIGHT
HORSE
BOOKS

Brighthorse Books
13202 N River Drive
Omaha, NE 68112

ISBN: 978-0-9908670-2-9

Cover Art: istockphoto © dapetheape
Author Photo: Erica Thibodeaux

For permission to reproduce selections from this book
and for more information about Brighthorse Books
and the Brighthorse Prize, visit us on the web at
brighthorsebooks.com.

For my students

"Specific knowledge is not education. . . . Education is learning how to live, and on what level. And you must learn that or everything else is useless."

James Salter, *Light Years*

LEAVING
MILAN

1

MILAN. IN OHIO, the emphasis was on the first part—
pronounced like "MY land" or "Mylar." The first time
Harper heard how it was said in other places—the emphasis
on the second syllable, open-ended—*Milan*, it sounded far-
off and elegant, a city of stone arches and turrets and cobble-
stones, a place she'd never know.

In early August the days floated, endless. The corn in the
distance grew, the lilies by the roadside flourished, star-like,
then closed. Cornflowers and Queen Anne's Lace dotted the
roadside on the way into town. Harper lay still, pretending to sleep, as her mother moved through the apartment,
getting ready for work. The scratch of a lighter, the closet
door opened and closed. Harper stretched, ducked her head
under the covers, then pressed her palms down the length
of her body. In the past year, she had filled out, becoming
petite and round at the same time. Her own supple softness
surprised her. The last time he was home, even David noticed the difference, joking that she'd turned from a carrot
into a peach. She felt delicate, as if she could bruise easily,

and hoped she would change as she got older: become more angled and defined.

The door closed and the apartment grew quiet. When she was sure her mother wouldn't come back for her keys or her wallet, Harper got out of bed, pulled on shorts and a T-shirt, and padded into the kitchen. Rings from her mother's coffee cup, like a squashed Olympic logo, had dried on the table. Cigarette smoke hung in the air. Harper walked to the sink and picked up a sponge floating in the gray water. She wrung it out; how could plastic, or whatever sponges were made of, smell so disgusting? She let the water run to hot, rinsed out the sponge, and wiped down the table. The bitter smell lingered on her hands, so she set the sponge in the sink, reached into the cabinet for baking soda and poured some onto the sponge. It would only help for a while. She would buy a new sponge today. "Happy fucking birthday," she muttered.

She edged into her flip-flops and opened the front door. Their apartment, on the second floor, had a cement walkway with a metal railing in front, which ran the length of the building. She slapped down the steps, the day already hot, the smell of oil rising from the parking lot. A bank of mailboxes, a metal grid of possibility and emptiness, stood in the corner. A tiny key opened their box. Nothing. She doubted she'd hear from her father. David wouldn't forget.

Harper surveyed the horizon. The white sky was empty; the buzz of the freeway hummed in her ears. Her friends had jobs: Katie was a chambermaid at the Motel 6; Janet worked at the old folks' home in Sandusky. Harper had tried to get work, but Sandusky was too far to walk, and the Motel 6 didn't need anyone. A new shopping center, close to her apartment, was supposed to open last year, but the project had stalled, so there weren't the jobs she'd hoped for.

She'd spent the summer reading library books, cleaning the apartment, and seeing Katie and Janet when they were off work. Whenever she went out, she washed her hair, put on make-up, shaved her arms and legs so that, in shorts and a tank top, she was aware of all her smoothness, her calves and thighs and arms. Her straight coppery hair brushed her shoulders. She was preparing for something without knowing what it was. Each day, she hoped for an adventure, and each day, it didn't happen. Like the horizon, it was always there, before her.

She scanned the road for the mail truck. The sky, attenuated blue, whitened in the heat. The mailman sometimes joked with her as he stuffed the mailboxes, claiming to be surprised that a pretty girl would talk to him. She didn't think of herself as pretty, although her friends called her that. Her face was oval, her eyes more gray than blue, and she had what her mother called a ski-jump nose, a bend in the middle, as if it pointed to something definite she would become.

Her front teeth were slightly crooked. The dentist had said that braces would be cosmetic rather than necessary, so her teeth were left alone.

Finally, when it was clear the mail wouldn't be early, she went inside, showered, brushed her hair and her teeth, then walked up the road to the new Dunkin' Donuts. She wanted to be on the top of the list when they started hiring. It was just a mile away, an easy walk. She walked past Chi Chi's, Outback Steak House, Taco Bell. The smell of fast food blended with car exhaust. People honked or hollered as they drove by, people who didn't know her. She kicked a clod of dirt and stepped over hummocks of dusty grass. No sidewalks. Nobody walked here, but she did. They'd been working on the Dunkin' Donuts building for weeks, the windows masked by white swirls like a woman's face hidden by cold cream.

Today, the windows were clean. A banner waved out front, "We're Open!" A chime sounded when Harper walked in; the smell of sugar washed over her. In late morning, the store was gleaming and empty. A man with a florid complexion and a stringy, black comb-over pushed through the swinging doors.

"What can I get for you today?"

"I'd like to apply for a job," she said.

"High school student?"

She nodded.

"You have to be reliable, show up for every shift." He reached under the counter for an application, then pushed the pad toward her, his wedding band tight around his pudgy finger.

Harper hiked herself up on a stool and filled out the application in handwriting as clear as she could manage. She brushed her hair out of her eyes.

"Are you hiring now?"

"You don't hardly look seventeen."

"I am." She pointed to a spot in the pad. "Today."

The man looked at her. "So you're serious about work."

"I sure am."

"If you miss a shift, I fire you."

"I won't miss," she said.

•

SHE TOOK HER time walking home. Milan, Ohio. Birthplace of Thomas Edison. A tiny red square in the Rand McNally atlas. People stopped here because there was nothing else on this stretch of interstate between Toledo and Cleveland. Almost every year, on a class trip, a teacher dragged them to the Edison birthplace, where they surveyed the little house and its inventions, smelled the old wood and linen, climbed the narrow steps to see the mother's button shoes and old-fashioned clothes. They jostled each other in line, picked at mosquito bites, joked about the fact that Edison had barely gone to school. They gazed dutifully at the sampler sewn by Edison's sister. Once, a doughy guide had commented that Edison's sister had trouble with spelling, and Anna Beth Polacheck had pointed out that his sister could spell just fine—those *f*s were actually old-fashioned *s*'s. The guide blushed below her frosted curls and said she would research it. Anna Beth shook her head in disgust.

The canal that had made Milan a thriving trade town was covered with vines and earth. The town was pretty in places, but its sense of liveliness was gone. Harper and her mother lived near the interstate, near the feed plant and the new Motel 6. She felt as if she'd been dropped in the wrong place and, just as a soldier dropped behind enemy lines could not stay where he landed, she had no intention of staying in Milan.

Cars rushed by as she stepped over torn McDonald's containers, Dairy Queen cups, mangled bendy straws. She wanted to live somewhere pretty and clean. Of course, there were picturesque parts of Milan: the town square surrounded by Victorian houses, antique stores with mansard roofs, but she knew from the way Matt's mother looked at her, from the way that people who knew her own mother looked at her, that she would never move to a nicer neighborhood.

One more year of school, and then she'd be free. Most of her friends said they'd go somewhere else after graduation, but the closest place was Sandusky, at the southern end of Lake Erie, the shoreline polluted by the cities to the north. Harper wanted to live where the smell of feed and asphalt didn't hang in the air.

The manager at Dunkin' Donuts called the next day and offered her a job. He said she'd have to do two orientation shifts without pay. Harper said she could start right away.

When she came in for her first shift, Dwight greeted her gravely and put his hand on her shoulder, welcoming her to the Dunkin' Donuts family. Harper tried to keep a straight face.

"Let's start in the back," Dwight said, "and work our way to the front. You're being hired to serve people, but you need to know where things are."

Harper followed him through the double doors. In the kitchen, the equipment and stainless steel counters shone. She liked the newness of the place, the smell of sugar and baking. Dwight explained what the different machines did, and the two men running them nodded to her without speaking. The men were short and dark, not much taller than Harper. In the stockroom, Dwight explained how the supplies were arranged; his mouth moved like a claymation character's. Under the counters, the brick-colored tile was clean. The orderliness, the rules about how long things could sit before they had to be thrown away, all made sense.

Dwight got her a hat and apron, showed her how to work the cash register, then let her stay up front. It was a relief to get away from his talk. Anyone could do this: making coffee, re-stocking donuts, keeping things clean. She wiped the counters and cleaned fingerprints off the donut cases. She had to have money, and her mother didn't have any, and her brother didn't have any, so she had to save up and get some for herself, something to get away on. She dreamed of a car, but David had told her, "Forget it, insurance and repairs'll soak up any money you get. Save up, get away from Mom, move to a place where you don't need a car."

David was at school in Madison. Harper had never been there, but it sounded pretty.

Madison. A girl's name. She imagined brick buildings with white pillars, green lawns, teenagers playing Frisbee by a lake.

Three years ago, the day he told her he was going, was their only real fight. David said he had something important to tell her, and they stood on the walkway outside the apartment, leaning on the railing.

"Listen, I got some good news. I got into the University of Wisconsin in Madison. I'm starting at the end of August."

The March sky was patchy gray, light clouds on top of dark ones. The dumpster in the corner of the lot, which David had spray-painted with curse words when he was younger, had become a graffiti art project, swirled with words and symbols, scraped and banged. David breathed out, slowly. She knew he wanted a cigarette. He pretended he didn't smoke because he didn't want her to start.

"Don't leave me alone with her."

"It's only a few years, and you'll be gone yourself."

"I can't stand it. You're the one she likes."

She saw in his eyes, in the set of his mouth, that protesting would be useless. Harper started to cry. Reaching forward, he pulled a strand of hair from her mouth. The wet strands of hair tugged on her lips.

"Harper, I have to go. I have to get out of here."

She turned and walked into the apartment, slamming the door behind her.

Dwight said she was a quick study, although Harper couldn't imagine what was hard to understand. *Get away, get away*, she chanted as she walked back and forth to work. Her classmates claimed they would leave for Chicago or Columbus or Cleveland. Katie said she'd go to college because her parents would make her, but she really wanted to buy a Victorian house in Milan itself. She wanted a house with a turret and a round bedroom. She planned to travel to estate sales, buy antiques, and open a shop of her own. Janet thought she might want to be a nurse.

Harper stopped at the mailbox, pulled out bills, advertisements, a birthday card from David, a day late. She wrote him letters because her mother didn't want her running up the phone bill. He always called her back, sometimes at night after he'd been out with his friends. Then his voice was urgent, as if his grown-up self was peeled back, revealing the brother she'd grown up with.

"You can't let Mom get to you. You have to imagine there's bulletproof glass, like Plexiglass between you. Say it to yourself while she's talking: *Plexiglass, Plexiglass, Plexiglass.* Imagine her words bounce off you."

Harper thought of it as a magic charm, like a cross to ward off vampires or the vial the elf princess gives Sam in the *Lord of the Rings*. It didn't sound magical—*Plexiglass, Plexiglass, Plexiglass*—but since David said it, she believed it would work.

The last time he was home, he'd helped her open a checking account. They'd gone to the bank, stood in the beige carpeted room amidst advertisements for mortgages and CDs, and filled out the paperwork together. "I get the free cooler they're offering." David grinned as he filled out the signature card. He was tan from his summer landscaping job; the tendons in his forearms moved as he wrote. On his left forearm was a burn mark from when he was a child. The patch of soft skin, almost the size of her palm, didn't tan. The pale skin gleamed, the one place their coloring was alike. Where David was blond and tan, Harper had her mother's fair skin and reddish hair. She tried to stay out of the sun so she wouldn't freckle.

"Put everything you can in here," David said. "Since I'm the co-signer, Mom can't take anything out. This is for you."

She was up to $87.26. She'd carried a deposit slip to Dunkin' Donuts on her first paid day of work and asked Dwight to have her paychecks deposited in her account. He had looked at her approvingly.

"It's so my mother can't cash them," Harper explained.

·

THE FIRST TIME Harper saw him, he came into Dunkin' Donuts late, with a friend. His dark brown hair was pulled back in a ponytail. He was slim and wore round, wire-framed glasses, a skinny leather bracelet on his wrist. His Phish T-shirt, faded green, didn't match his striped cloth shorts and sandals. His friend was gangly, with bright acne scars, and wore a headband over his straight blond hair. They looked like college students, but there was no college close by.

They ordered coffee, then stood in front of the donut case, pulling money, colored string, keys, and trinkets, out of their pockets. The tall boy, the one with acne scars, started laughing. "Clown car in my pocket. Neee neee nee ooouuuneee!" He waved his arm in a circle, playing the air guitar. Harper smiled. He reached for one of the objects he'd set on the counter, turned a small plastic knob, and set a piece of pink plastic chattering across the counter. She couldn't imagine what it was and looked at him, puzzled. "Mobile sushi," he giggled, then laughed as the toy spun and stalled in the change. "This calls for the antidote: something with custard!"

They studied the cases—crullers or raised donuts, glazed or filled, jelly or cream, sprinkles or sugar or chocolate—weighing their choices. She waited for the brown-haired boy to speak.

"No custard. I like the plain ones." He pushed his glasses up his nose.

"Dude, you're weird," the tall boy said. He bent down to peer into the cases, then pointed to a row of donuts. Harper started to reach for one. "No, wait a second," he said, then pointed to something else, and she moved toward that. "No, wait." He seemed amused by the ordering process, as if it were surprising that Harper would reach for what he pointed to, as if they didn't speak the same language.

The bells chimed and a family walked in the door. The brown-haired boy looked over his shoulder.

"Paco, she's got stuff to do. Order what you want."

Harper smiled at him. Paco ordered fancies and donuts with sprinkles.

The dark-haired boy asked for a glazed donut and a cruller. His voice was low and solemn. Harper felt as if she were offering food to an animal, careful not to startle him, as she handed him his donuts and his change.

When they had their donuts and took their seats, the brown-haired boy set a thick notebook, covered with wavy lines, on the counter. Harper waited on the family who'd just come in and, as the youngest boy negotiated with his mother, and his sisters fussed, it took them forever to choose a dozen donuts. When she finally boxed the donuts, got the parents coffee, and made change, she moved down the counter to look at his book. The cover was swirled with soft gray lines, like waves of spilled oil on white water. She leaned over to examine it.

"Suminagashi," he said.

"What?"

"It's a Japanese form of decorating paper."

She didn't understand, but tried to look as if she did.

"I made the designs on the paper, then covered the notebook with it."

"You put the paper on yourself?" She touched the cover, neat and tight, like something from a store.

"Yeah."

"How do you do it?"

"The suminagashi? It's like marbling paper. You take a big flat tray, fill it with water, and you drop paint on top of the water. Then you use a straw, or a comb, to swirl patterns in the paint. Then, pretty quickly, you lay a piece of paper on top of it and the paint sticks to the paper."

Paco plucked a straw from the dispenser on the counter. He stuck the straw into a jelly donut, drew in his cheeks, made a great show of pretending to suck the jelly out, then turned to his friend and said, "It's ready now, dude."

The brown-haired boy laughed, held onto the counter, growing red in the face; they both doubled over, laughing so hard they were gasping for air. Paco slid off his stool, falling onto the floor, which made them laugh even harder.

She turned to wait on two girls who'd just come in, checked the coffee, and saw to the next batch of donuts coming out. They must be stoned. When they'd finally recovered, and eaten their donuts, they seemed reluctant to leave.

"Where are you from?" Harper wiped the counter next to his book and tried to make the question sound casual.

"My family's from Akron, but I'm going back to Oly."

"Where?"

"Olympia, Washington."

"What's it like there?"

"It's nice. College town and all. It's pretty alternative."

"Alternative to what?"

He looked around him. She tried to see it as he did. Gleaming metal. Plastic and glass. "Alternative to this."

"Oh." She wasn't sure whether to be offended or not.

"What's your name?"

"Harper."

"Harper, cool. I'm Nate."

2

TECHNICALLY, HARPER ALREADY had a boyfriend, Matthew Douglas. She thought of him as a boyfriend-at-school, the boyfriend equivalent of a training bra. She hardly saw him over the summer; he worked as a caddy at the country club and, at his parents' insistence, was taking an SAT prep course. When he called on the phone, they quickly ran out of things to say.

Harper had gone to the prom with him because he'd asked her, but his admiration was annoying because he only knew the surface she presented to him. She never invited him home, and he'd only met her mother once: when Harper and her mother were grocery shopping. They ran into him at Krogers, where Matt was buying chips and salsa. Harper glanced at her mother, who looked tired, but not unkempt. Matt extended his hand, trying to act grown-up.

"You go to school with Harper?" Her mother ignored his hand and pursed her mouth.

"Yes, ma'am." Matt lowered his hand, then reached into his

pocket, as if this would hide his original gesture.

"Well, nice to meet you," she said and pushed her cart forward, as if she had just seen something important in the frozen food aisle.

Later, he said, "Your mother doesn't seem so bad."

"You don't really know her," Harper said.

Harper had seen *Leave it to Beaver* on Nick at Nite, and if Matt could be plunked into the nineteen-fifties, he would feel at home. He was one of the popular kids because his father was successful. She guessed that he liked the way her blonde-red hair fell against her shoulders, her ski-jump nose, the way she looked in a tank top. He didn't see her mother's nicotine-stained fingers, her puckered lips, the missing teeth on the side of her mouth. He took it for granted that Harper would go away to college, and his attention seemed a sign she could escape, become a different person.

Last spring, Matt had invited her over for a family picnic. The Douglas's house was large and clean, not far from the high school, and it looked like a picture in a magazine. They played badminton and croquet on the huge back lawn. Matt's younger brother and sister had invited friends too, and Mrs. Douglas served them cookies and chips, and Pepsi in tall plastic glasses meant just for picnics and cookouts. The casual gathering made Harper edgy, as if her true self couldn't help but leak through.

Sometimes, when she went over to Matt's, his mother made them a snack after school, although it could hardly be called a snack, more what seemed like a meal. She made them sandwiches or dished out pasta salad. Mrs. Douglas would go on and on about how teenage boys could eat, fluttering over Matt, smoothing his T-shirt, resting her elaborately ringed fingers on his shoulder as she spoke. Matt shrugged her off and asked Harper if she'd like anything else.

"I'd better go along to work," Mrs. Douglas said. When

she smiled at Harper, her mouth turned up at the corners, but her eyes narrowed. "The store can be busy on Friday afternoon, tourists and all. I'm glad it's just part-time, I do it to get out," she explained.

Harper smiled as if she understood. She imagined her mother mimicking Mrs. Douglas: *I do it to get out.* Harper knew what her mother really thought: *Miss Fancy Pants screwed her way into that fancy house, just likes to rub people's noses in the fact that she doesn't have to work.* Mrs. Douglas had been a year ahead of Harper's mother in high school, a fact that shocked Harper when she learned it, because Matt's mother looked so much younger. She sensed a caution, a scrutiny in Mrs. Douglas, which she didn't understand, until one day last spring, when she'd gone home with Matt after school.

They'd come in the back door, and Matt went to use the bathroom, leaving Harper alone in the shining kitchen. His mother was on the phone in the next room.

"Well, you know, I try to be kind. She's a nice girl, and she's trying to do well for herself, but you know her mother...."

There was quiet as she listened to the reply.

"Well, I'm trying to give her the benefit of the doubt. Her brother's at college in Madison, and it's hard to get in out of state, so there must be some brains in the family. I think they're all on Bill's side though."

A hot tingling pricked Harper's neck. The row of copper pots, in graduated sizes, blurred on the wall. A grown-up was talking about her. Unbelievable. She opened the cabinet where the glasses were kept, let the door close loudly, then turned on the tap. There must be some brains ... all on Bill's side. She ran the water, letting it run cold over her hands, and decided that she'd do it. She'd have sex with Matt, right in his own house, while his mother was out.

She'd been thinking about it anyway. Matt wanted to. She'd heard it wasn't very good the first time, and she wanted to get it over with. Matt wouldn't argue about using a condom. He'd probably practiced.

She made Matt wait for a day when his mother would be out, taking his brother and sister to some after-school sport. It would have been easier to do at her apartment, while her mother was at work, but Harper didn't want to do it there. She felt like they were lab partners working on an experiment whose objective wasn't completely clear. They walked home from school, over to his house, talking about nothing, and Harper ran her fingers along the smooth bannister as they climbed the stairs, the hallway above filled with photos of the Douglas children holding ribbons or trophies, wearing plaid shorts or tennis shirts, grinning toothily. Matt's bedroom, filled with baseball memorabilia and sports equipment, was dark in the afternoon. Harper's chest felt tight; she wished she could change her mind.

Taking off her clothes felt like getting changed for gym class. They got into Matt's unmade bed, the wood headboard and sharp smell of sweaty sheets enveloping her, and she sank into the shadowed light. His arms were smooth and taut from working out, and she ran her fingers down the lines of them, wanting a motion to convey what she could not say. His breathing was thick and congested, and he tried to talk, to tell her she was pretty, but his words, thick and garbled, meant nothing. She tried to relax. He tore open a rubber, rolled it on carefully. His penis looked strange covered in latex, the soft skin sealed away. She thought of Boy Scouts, merit badges, what if they gave out merit badges for practicing with condoms?

Something in her trembled; she couldn't laugh. Over his

shoulder, baseball pennants on the wall hung like daggers. Matt touched her, but he pressed too hard, and it felt uncomfortable and weird, not good at all. Mostly, it was strange, alien, that she let him do this to her. The whole thing didn't take very long. When it was over, Matt was damp and grateful.

•

NATE CAME BACK to Dunkin' Donuts the next night, alone. "I wanted to know if you felt like going out later on," he said. "There's a party in Sandusky tonight."

"I don't have a car," she said.

"I do."

She peered through the window as if she were deciding.

"If you can't, it's okay. We stopped here 'cause Paco has a cousin up in Sandusky. I don't know anyone. I just thought I'd ask."

"I'd like to," she said. "I'd like to hear about Olympia. What's it like there?"

"The greenest place you've never seen."

"I'm done at ten," she said.

•

THEY CAME TO pick her up a few hours later. Harper felt slender and smooth, perched between Nate and Paco in the front of the truck. She was aware of them on either side, the way Nate had to reach across her thigh to shift, the tan muscles of his arm, Paco's long legs. Paco sang to whatever came on the radio and beat on the dashboard with a pair of chopsticks. At stoplights, when someone pulled up next to them, he'd look over and grin, beat an elaborate drum roll on the dash.

The party was at a small house on the outskirts of Sandusky. A small crowd stood on the porch, drinking beer, talking and laughing; music pulsed from inside. Nate parked the truck down the street, and they walked towards the dark throb of a bass. Honeysuckle and pot drifted through the night air, mixing with a thin current of cigarette smoke, like swimming in a lake and suddenly hitting a cold spot. Paco grinned, sniffing the air like a retriever, and moved toward the house.

Inside, they moved through the crowd, found the keg and some cups. Paco disappeared in search of his cousin.

"Do you want to go back outside?" Nate shouted over the noise.

"Sure." Harper lifted her beer above her head, felt him following her as they pressed through the crowded house.

Across the street, a busted-up picnic table marked the edge of what had once been a park. The swings were gone; only the frame remained. Relieved to be away from the grinding noise, she walked towards the picnic table.

"So what made you move to Olympia?"

"I was going to Evergreen for a while, but I decided to take some time off."

"What's Evergreen?"

"It's a college. It's the kind of place where you can design your own major, that kind of thing."

She pulled a frayed thread in the knee of her jeans. "So what do you do now?"

"Work at a bike shop. Paco does too. Actually, he's got this side thing going—he makes smoothies without electricity. He pedals his bike to get the blender going. He does it at street fairs and stuff."

"You're kidding."

"Nope."

"I'm sorry, but that's ridiculous."

"Well, that's part of it. People buy the smoothies partly because they can't believe he does it that way."

"People aren't like that here."

"I can tell."

His voice was low, a little flat; it was hard to tell whether he was amused or not.

A street lamp on the corner made the night electric blue. She wanted to see him in daylight, to read his expression. Her impression was that he was handsome, but he hid it behind a scraggly beard and long hair.

"I'm saving up to leave," she said.

"For where?"

"I don't know. My brother's at school at Madison."

"Cool town."

"Everything here is dirty." The park's littered sandbox, the swing set bordered by weeds, seemed like an extension of home. Powerlines ranged behind the party house with its sagging porch.

A couple was making out against the brick wall of the building next to the party, and Nate half-turned so they wouldn't face them. "You'd like Olympia. I can picture you there."

He could imagine her someplace else. How would she describe him to Janet or Katie? A hippie college kid. Deep brown eyes. The outer shell, what other people saw, seemed young and ineffectual, but some other part of him seemed wise.

"Everyone here talks about leaving, but no one does. Or if they leave, they go to Chicago or Cleveland. I don't want to go to a city."

"So your parents live here?"

"My mom does. She works at a car graveyard." Harper pictured the paneling, the girlie calendars. "She fits right in. What are your parents like?"

"Pretty mainstream. They're real Christian, so they think I'm weird, but they're okay. They're bummed I'm not in school now. I came home because my grandmother was sick, and then she kind of rallied, but my mom still thought I should come home. Part of the plan was that my dad gave me his old pickup truck, which was really cool of him." Nate looked over the rooftops, in the direction of the powerlines. "We're staying tomorrow night and then going on. Paco says there's a rave up here tomorrow. Want to go?"

"Why not?" Harper said.

•

ON WEEKEND NIGHTS, Harper's mother came in late. Through the wall, Harper heard her go into the bathroom, open the cabinet for aspirin, get some water, and trudge back to bed. She slept till noon. The first time her mother didn't come home was the fall that David went away to college. Harper woke on a sunny Saturday morning and realized the apartment was empty. A slow, hot fear overtook her. What if her mother had been in an accident? Harper curled under her blankets; dust motes swam in the sunlight. Who would she belong to if her mother died? Would her father come and get her?

She got out of bed and walked down the hall to the phone. She was dialing the hospital when her mother, still in last night's clothes, walked in the door.

Harper set down the phone.

"I was calling the emergency room."

"Oh, please," her mother said. "You worry too much. I need a shower. Make me some coffee, will you?"

She dropped her purse and jacket on a chair. Harper put water on to boil. In the time it took her mother to shower, Harper felt foolish, then angry. She went out for a walk, although there was really no place to go, leaving a cup of coffee on the counter.

After that, her mother would occasionally bring someone

home with her. Harper hated finding an unexpected man in the apartment: a sharp smell, something peppery and male and inchoate. Occasionally, Harper heard her mother getting someone up and out when she got up for her water and aspirin.

•

SATURDAY MORNING. THE hum of the refrigerator and the freeway in the distance. Harper got up to use the bathroom; her mother's bedroom door was open—no one there. Harper decided to stay up, so she'd be dressed and starting the day when her mother came in. It would give her an advantage when she asked about going out that night.

Harper dialed Janet's cell phone.

"Hullo?" Janet sounded as if she'd barely woken up.

"You remember those guys I told you about?"

"Yeah, sure."

"They asked if we wanted to go to a rave up in Sandusky."

"What're they like?"

"Kind of granola-heads, but nice."

Janet giggled. "But they're not weird?"

"Not bad weird. You know, tie-dye and stuff. Last night, Paco was wearing a T-shirt that said, 'Visualize whirled peas.'"

"What?"

"It's a joke."

"I don't get it."

"Never mind. I hate your cell phone. We'll come up to Sandusky and meet you after work, okay?"

Harper was eating toast when her mother came in the front door. In summer's warmth there was no coat to hang up, no gloves or hat to put away, to shield the awkwardness of her arrival. Her mother put the kettle on the stove. She wore a short-sleeved shirt with a swirling pattern of pink and black, a pair of polyester pants. Yesterday's work clothes. She put two teaspoons of Taster's Choice in a mug and gazed out the window as she waited for the water to boil.

Harper was glad she didn't look like her mother. She'd seen pictures of her father and recognized her bow-shaped mouth in his. She did have her mother's straight, coppery hair, although her mother's was now short and shot with gray. Harper found it hard to believe she was once part of her mother, who was desiccated and gloomy, incapable of carrying anything live and liquid inside her.

"I got a job at the Dunkin' Donuts."

Her mother plopped down at the kitchen table. Her charm bracelet rattled as she stirred her coffee. "When was that?"

"This week."

"Good for you."

"I'm working tonight until ten. Then I'm going over to Janet's. She said I could stay the night."

Her mother stopped stirring and took a sip. "What's Janet driving?"

"Her mother lets her use the car if she doesn't need it. That's how she gets back and forth to Sandusky."

"I don't like the idea of you walking along the road when you get off at night."

"I know, I'm careful. I stay off to the side."

Her mother lit a cigarette. "I can't afford to get you a car so you can get back and forth to a minimum wage job."

"I know."

Her mother's expression relaxed as she smoked and drank her coffee. The skin above her eyes was papery and translucent.

"Mom?"

Her mother looked up, wary.

"Why did we stay here?"

"What?"

Harper took a breath. She knew better than to say, 'after Dad left.' "After you and Dad split up, why didn't you go somewhere different?"

Her mother sighed. "Christ, I'm not even awake yet." She tapped her cigarette in the ashtray and looked past Harper. "I don't know. After your uncle died, there was no one else to take care of your Nana. I knew that would be on me. And where would I go? Your father was always wanting to get out of here, but I grew up here. This is home."

"But you always complain about it here."

"Well, I might complain, but at least I know the score. The main problem is jobs, finding one with decent pay." Her mother set her chin, the skin under her jaw now loose and rumpled. "I thought things might pick up here. Maybe with Six Flags coming in there'd be a new mall in Sandusky, but nothing ever took off. Your brother was smart to get out."

"This is the year I apply to colleges too."

"Your brother is the smart one."

"My grades are fine."

"Fine won't get you a scholarship."

"I can still try."

"I can still try." Her mother mimicked her plaintive tone. "Try away. It's good you got a job. You can start saving up."

Harper went to take a shower. In the bathroom she stripped and studied herself in the mirror. People sometimes said she looked like a singer, Avril Lavigne, back when she was a skater girl. Harper didn't think so; her own face was less pointed, but when people pointed out the resemblance, secretly, she was pleased. They were both small, with the same straight, coppery hair. They had the same kind of body. Janet was openly envious. "You're tiny and you have real tits—it's so not fair." Janet wore hip-huggers because she thought they were in fashion, but her flesh pushed over the top of her belt. She wore odd barrettes that no one could talk her out of—plastic baby barrettes, slender bobby pins with sparkles—her barrettes had become a running joke. Whenever her friends found a particularly odd or goofy pair, they gave them to Janet, who plunked them over her shiny forehead and grinned. Harper and Janet had been friends since second grade. Next to David, Harper loved her more than anyone.

•

HARPER RODE UP to Sandusky with Nate and Paco that night. She had chosen a deep blue top with spaghetti straps, a silky pale blue bra underneath, her favorite pair of jeans. She was excited for Janet to meet them. The crazy things Nate talked about—paper-making, food co-ops, Paco and his smoothies—confirmed what she had hoped: there were places where people were different. In Milan, calling something 'different' was a cut. If someone said, 'Well, that's different,' you knew it was bad. Harper thought it should be the opposite: since normal was boring, different could be good.

In the long days of summer, the sky was still light, a pale blue deepening to azure. The old folks' home where Janet worked was a highrise building with a park-like lawn. Set on the banks of Lake Erie, it looked like a fancy hotel. Some people got jobs there after graduating. Behind the highrise, dotting the shoreline, signs warned people not to swim in the water. The parking lot was full near the building, so they parked at the far end of the lot.

When Janet came out of the building, she didn't see them at first, and Harper saw her as a stranger might: a slightly thickened girl with light brown hair in a blunt cut to her shoulders. Her barrettes, high on her forehead, looked like a city girl wearing bobby pins as a retro move, but Janet's style wasn't urban enough to convey that sense of irony, so she simply looked goofy.

Harper got out of the truck and waved. As Janet ambled toward them, Paco and Nate gathered a few plastic lawn chairs scattered on the edge of the grounds. Janet giggled as she came up. "I've never seen anyone use these chairs. Most of our clients can't walk this far."

"This is my friend, Janet," Harper said.

Paco grinned and gestured that Janet should have a seat.

The sky grew pink at the horizon. Gulls plucked at debris on the shore. Paco studied the warning signs along the shoreline.

"Water's pretty polluted, huh?" Paco said.

"I suppose. No one really says what's wrong."

"It's like that Michael Moore movie," Nate said.

"What?"

"You know, where he follows people around and tries to get them to talk."

"I don't know what you're talking about," Janet said.

"Doofus and me," Paco said.

"What?"

"*Roger and Me*," Nate clarified.

"*No comprendez*," Janet said.

"This guy, Michael Moore, made a movie about trying to get the Chairman of General Motors to talk to him. He walked all around Detroit with a movie camera, went to this fancy men's club he belonged to, and of course the guy wouldn't talk to him, but he went all round—"

"The chairman?"

"No, the guy making the movie. He went to places in Detroit where people worked in car factories all their lives and lost their jobs and were being kicked out of their apartments and stuff. It really sucked," Nate said.

"You guys are really serious types," Janet said.

"So what happened in the end?" Harper asked.

"Well, nothing really."

"But that was kind of the point; there was nothing they

could do," Paco said.

Harper knew they'd brought it up because the desolation was the same here. Anyone could see things wouldn't get better.

"Where are you guys from?" Janet asked.

"Oly's home," Paco said. "But I grew up outside Cleveland. Nate told me he had to come out, so I got a cheap flight too. I thought it would be cool to drive back. I want to stop in the Badlands, then buzz back home. Really, I'd like to do it on a bike, but there's another route I want to do first."

"What's that?"

"I want to bike up to Vancouver and back."

Janet nodded, and Harper chewed the inside of her lip, hoping that Janet wouldn't ask where Vancouver was. Harper knew it was in Canada, although she wasn't sure exactly where.

Their conversation stalled, and they looked toward the lake. Dark had started to fall. "Let's check out the party," Janet said. "How did you hear about it?"

"I have a cousin who lives here," Paco said. "I don't know him that well, but he said we could crash here."

Since they couldn't all fit in the front of Nate's truck, Harper rode in Janet's car, and they followed Nate and Paco.

"They seem nice," Janet said. "Paco's funny."

"I told my mom I was staying at your house tonight."

"No problem." Janet bounced in her seat as they drove. "They're cute, they party. I can't believe you met them at Dunkin' Donuts."

"They were stoned."

"I bet."

"What do you think about Nate?"

"I bet he's cute under that scruffy beard. He seems serious, though."

"He is, kind of." Up ahead, Harper could see Nate slowing down, signaling a right turn. "Here it is." Harper pointed.

Janet followed them down an access road then pulled into the back of a half-full parking lot. The rave was at an old brick building, an abandoned sewing factory, on the shore. They eased through the lot; people gathered in the dusk—smoking, talking, laughing—in small groups around parked cars. A crowd had already gathered outside the building. Janet parked next to Nate's truck and they all got out and walked together across the parking lot. Harper felt a nervous expectation as they moved into the back of the crowd. Paco and Janet dug in their pockets. It cost twenty dollars to get in. Harper looked at Nate. She had ten dollars, but even if she had enough, she didn't want to spend it. Everything was measured in increments of getting away.

"Do you want to go in?" Nate asked.

"Isn't there beer in the truck?"

"We'll come in later," Nate said to Paco.

Janet looked at Harper.

"We'll see you later on," Harper said.

They got back into Nate's truck, and he drove it to the north side of the parking lot, facing the lake. Blue on blue, the sky dimmed over the water. They sat in the truck, sipping beer, looking at the lights blinking in the distance.

"What are those?" Nate pointed to a few small lights on the horizon.

"I think it's Marblehead, or Kelley's Island."

"Have you ever been there?"

"No."

"It's not very far."

"My mother doesn't like going anywhere, and I don't have a way to get there myself." She studied the line of his arm. "So, what are you going to do when you go back to Olympia?"

"I don't know. I can always go back to the bike shop, but I might apply for a job at the food co-op. Health benefits and all.

I could join Americorps, it'd help pay for school."

"What's Americorps?"

He explained about the benefits for tuition, the different jobs his friends had done, how they worked outdoors. "I'd like to try living without electricity for a while. I have some friends who said I could live in their yurt."

"A yurt?"

"Do you know what it is?"

She shook her head.

"It's got a cool shape. They're originally from Siberia." He reached across her and pulled a small pad from the glove compartment. With a fine-tipped pen, he drew a rounded, tent-like structure, wider at the bottom than the top. His lines were quick and sure, his hands relaxed, as if drawing were reflexive, easy as speaking. She leaned closer to look, letting her hair fall on his shoulder.

"What about a bathroom? A shower?"

"Outhouse. I suppose I'd have to hit up friends for showers."

She shook her head. "That's crazy," she said, but it came out fondly, amused. "You could really live in a yurt?"

"For a while, why not?" He smelled clean, like peppermint. He flipped over the page and a small piece of colored paper fell out.

"What's that?"

"I'm teaching myself origami."

He bent over the small piece of yellow paper, set it on the pad, folded it several times, more quickly than she could follow, then held it in his palm. A tiny swan.

"How did you do that?"

"Want me to show you?"

He took her through the steps, but it was harder than it looked; her fingers felt large and clumsy.

"It's okay. It just takes practice. Let me show you." He leaned toward her again, reaching under the passenger seat. She wanted to run her hand down his back. The scent of peppermint again. He pulled a cigar box from under the seat and passed it to her. The box was filled with swans, all in different colors.

"What are you going to do with them?"

"I don't know, they're just for practice, really."

He picked out a mango-colored swan and placed it in her palm. They were quiet for a few minutes. She held the box of tiny swans in her lap.

Their conversation wandered for hours. Harper felt she could say things to him about the kind of life she wanted, things that wouldn't make sense to Janet or Katie.

"My brother really likes school. My mother always says he's the smart one. I don't know what I want to study. I don't know about anything really—high school subjects."

"You seem pretty smart to me."

She touched his hand with her finger, a silent thanks. "This Americorps thing pays enough to live on?"

"Not a lot, but yeah."

The beer was making her sleepy. They'd been talking for hours and exhausted what they could easily say. He leaned over and kissed her softly. Too softly. She kissed him back. The stick shift and gearbox were between their legs.

"Do you want to get in back and lie down?" Nate asked.

She put her hand on the door handle and pushed.

The pickup had a camper shell with a mattress in back. The bed was neatly made; the sheets must have come from his family, a brown and orange pattern that looked like something from the seventies, but clean, with a Mexican blanket on top. He took off his glasses and set them on his backpack, which rested against another pack at the head of the truck. They lay down, facing each other.

"When we didn't go into the rave, I didn't mean we had to —"

"I know."

"It's too bad you have one more year of school. You could come with me."

She searched his face, looking for some sign of flippancy or teasing. "We don't know each other."

"I know. But I think you'd like it out there. You could come along, and if you didn't like it, you could come back."

She ran her fingers over his cheekbones, his throat, which seemed boyish, but tensile and strong. He knew the resonance of the world, without knowing the world itself.

"My mother doesn't care that I'm around, but if I took off, I think she'd try to get me back. When I leave, I want to make sure I don't have to come back."

He leaned back, his head on his arm, and studied her. She couldn't read his expression in the dark.

"I just meant that I'm applying to colleges this year. I need a game plan or a scholarship or something, so I don't get stuck here."

He rolled toward her, and they kissed for a long time, a wordless conversation. He kissed her neck, her throat, her shoulders, sliding the straps of her shirt down her arms. Inside, she was wet, aching.

She pulled away for a moment. The faint light from outside was silver; she could only see his outline in the chrome dark. She felt it: everything was changing. Paco and Janet wouldn't be back for hours. Janet had whispered, "Paco's got some ecstasy!" They'd be in there all night.

They kissed for a long time. Nate was better at it than Matt was. He was better at everything really. Matt had touched her as if he'd memorized a treasure map and had to find his way in the dark without knowing what he was looking for. Nate was different. He paid attention to her, rather than paying attention to what he guessed was the right thing to do. Slowly, he kissed her shoulders, her throat.

"Wait." She sat up for a moment, reached behind herself, and undid her bra. She pulled the knot of clothes off, over her head, and lay back down, shirtless in her jeans.

"Is this okay? Do you really want to?" Nate asked.

"I don't have any birth control."

"I do." He kissed her, long and hard, then unbuttoned the top of her jeans, unzipped them and, scooting to the back of the truck, tugged them off from the bottom. He slid his body over her as he reached for his backpack, and she ran her hands down his torso, pushed his boxers off his hips. She reached to touch him, his skin so soft, softer than she had imagined. He pulled a rubber from the front pouch of his backpack.

He knelt in front of her, putting it on. His hair had come loose from his ponytail and fell to his shoulders. He was beautiful. Naked, he wasn't as boyish as he seemed. Muscular and thin. He turned to her, and she felt they were in their own little world, their own cocoon, and still, he waited, and touched her, until she couldn't stand it anymore and pulled him toward her, and he finally put himself inside her.

Oh, it felt so much better than it did before. They didn't have to hurry. She opened her eyes to see him over her. He was looking down, smiling, and dipped down to kiss her throat.

He moved in her more quickly, and she watched his face as he looked up, moved faster. Then, "Oh shit," he said.

"What?"

"The rubber broke."

She couldn't feel any difference. "Don't worry."

He started to pull out of her.

"No, wait," she said. "It already broke. Just lie here, be still." She could feel him inside her, still hard. Then he trembled and softened inside her.

"I don't have any others."

"It doesn't matter." She ached with wanting, but it was an amazing sensation, that she could hold him in her arms and he could still be inside her. He rested his head on her breasts, and they stayed like that for a long time, her hands running through his hair.

·

WHEN THEY WOKE in the early morning, the air was cool and damp, a pearly fog off the lake. She lifted her fingers to her face: her hands smelled like sex. Outside, it was quiet, the music from the rave muted. They burrowed under the covers, and she ran her fingers across his chest. What would it feel like to leave with him and Paco? To simply not go back? Leave her mother behind? She hadn't even gotten a full paycheck yet. Judging from the coins they pulled from their pockets at Dunkin' Donuts, they probably didn't have much money either. If she had money, she could do as she wanted, but she couldn't just get into a truck, without any cash, with two boys she didn't know. She slipped a leg between his legs, nestled against him, and fell back to sleep.

When she woke again, she was thirsty. Nate pulled water bottles from a corner of the truck and handed one to her.

She sat up, tipped her head back and drank the water, cool and silvery. Nate lay on his side, watching her. She was aware of her nakedness, slender and perfect. She pushed back the covers.

"Do you know how pretty you are?" He sounded dazed.

"I like my feet," she announced. She pointed her toes, like a dancer, then relaxed them.

Last week she'd painted her toenails, but now their brightness seemed artificial, too bright against her nakedness.

"I have feet like shovels," Nate said.

She giggled. "What do you mean?"

He reached for his boxers, pulled them on, then sat up next

to her. "They're flat and rectangular." He stretched out his legs, which were muscled and hairy, so she could see.

"They look fine to me."

"I have this weird thing. My mom has it too." He bent his knee, bringing his foot closer, and pointed to the smallest toe on his right foot. "The toenail's split, almost in the middle. It's always been that way."

She studied his foot. "It just looks like a big hangnail."

"I know, but it grows that way."

"That's not so weird."

"I know." He smiled at her, then twisted around and dropped his face against her breasts.

"Oh, I wish you could come back to Olympia." He spoke into her soft flesh.

They were quiet together, and she ran her hands through his hair. Barely dawn. She couldn't go home too early; if her mother woke up, she would know that Harper hadn't spent the night at Janet's.

"I need caffeine," Nate said, "but I guess Paco's still in the rave."

He sat up, hair falling to his shoulders, and she touched it because she could now. He was muscular in a way that wasn't apparent in clothes. She ran her hand down his forearm then turned to look out the little window of the camper shell. The parking lot was still full; she couldn't remember where Janet had left the car.

"If we get coffee, we can just come back. We'll park next to Janet's car, and they'll find us."

"I forgot we moved."

She didn't want to leave their warmth. She shivered in the early morning and felt uncovered without him against her. She retrieved her shirt from the top of the bed, her underpants from near the tailgate.

"Do you have a sweatshirt I could borrow?"

He pulled a gray hooded sweatshirt that said Evergreen out of his knapsack. She admired his deftness—he traveled with little and knew where everything was. The sweatshirt was too big for her, and she huddled in its warmth. They got into the cab and drove around till they found a place to buy tea and coffee, then drove back to the rave, the sun barely up. They sat in the front of the truck, looking out at the mist rising off the lake.

He pulled the plastic lid off his tea. "There's almost a rainbow on the top of my tea. With all the signs about the water here, it makes me a little nervous." His tone was solemn.

"I hate it here," Harper said.

"Whenever I visit my family, I feel homesick for Olympia. I've only lived there for two years, but it just feels right."

"I'd like to feel homesick for somewhere," Harper said.

At the edge of the parking lot, a squirrel pulled a piece of bread off the grass and a gull, squawking, chased after it. The day was warming and Harper felt peculiarly satisfied. Janet would come back, and they would return to her house, shower, and Harper would get home with her mother none the wiser.

When Paco and Janet finally appeared at the truck, bleary-eyed, Harper felt like going back to sleep.

"Oh, man, I'm beat," Paco said.

Nate handed him a lukewarm cup of coffee.

"We better go," Janet said to Harper. "I told my mother we'd be late, but not all night. She pulled her cell phone out of her bag, then smirked. "She didn't call my cell. She's probably asleep. We can slip in and just say we came in late."

Janet turned and gave Paco a hug. "It was a great night. Thanks for the X."

Harper turned to Nate and stuck her hands in her pockets. She didn't want to mirror Janet. She stood still, felt the balls of her feet through her thin sneakers.

"Bye, have fun in your yurt."
He grinned.

•

HARPER THOUGHT ABOUT him with pleasure, like a happy memory that isn't expected to be repeated, and so doesn't create anxiety. In the awkwardness of their hurried good-bye, she'd forgotten to give him his sweatshirt, or not really forgotten, she hadn't wanted to give it back, and so was glad when he hadn't asked for it. Harper wore it in her bedroom, pulled the front up to her face so that her nose rested inside the soft cotton. He had smelled like peppermint, but the smell was on his skin, not his clothes, and she couldn't call it back. His kisses tasted like clean water. She imagined that she had gone with him, her soul rising out of her body and following, so that the girl in Milan was a stand-in, going through familiar motions, while her other self, her real self, inhabited a world of pine trees and water and sky.

Senior year, the door to leaving. As if on cue, the weather turned cool over Labor Day, and she felt a sense of life speeding up—everything would open in front of her. She would apply to colleges, borrow money if she had to, she would get out of Milan.

3

DAVID HAD BURNED a bunch of CDs and sent them to Harper. He'd labeled some with a Sharpie, but the handwriting on others was unfamiliar, as if some artsy girl had written on them. Harper slipped one into the CD player and turned it up. Her mother wouldn't be home for a while. She sang along to the tunes she recognized, thinking about Nate, wishing she'd gone with him.

Singing made her feel better. She'd sing in the school chorus if there was a way for her to get home late and it wasn't so dorky.

The apartment door closed. Harper jumped, then shut the CD player off.

Her mother set her purse on the kitchen table. "Tomorrow's karaoke night at Shorty's, they're having a big prize. You should come and do that song."

"I can't sing in front of people."

Her mother pulled a pizza out of the freezer. "Don't be a sourpuss. There's a prize. You could win a hundred dollars."

"Don't you have to be twenty-one to be in a bar?"

"You have to be twenty-one to drink. You could come in. Hap knows me. Really, you should do that song. I've seen that girl on MTV or whatever. You've got the same hair as her."

Harper plucked the tab on her soda can. When had her mother actually wanted to do something with her?

"Mom, I can't really sing. I'm just following the music."

"It doesn't matter. You look just like her! All you need is some make-up, you know, dark around the eyes."

"I'll think about it."

"It's tomorrow night." Her mother hummed as she pre-heated the oven, then turned on the CD player and played it again, jerking her hips to the music. Harper didn't sing along. She hoped her mother would forget about it.

•

THE FOLLOWING NIGHT, her mother came home early from happy hour. "You coming back out?"

"Mom, I don't think I can do it."

"Oh, come on! It'll be fun. Just come out, you don't have to sing. Just come and see."

Harper wished she could flip a switch inside herself, turn on enthusiasm. Her foot cramped, a sudden pain, and she stepped on the ball of her foot, bending the arch to make the cramp go away. She didn't want to stand up in front of a bunch of people, but her mother's good mood was so rare that Harper hated to discourage it. The apartment, with its brown shag rug, the TV on mute, was oppressive. She could sit here alone, flip through old magazines for the millionth time, or she could go out.

"I'm not promising I'll do it." Harper knew it was a mistake, even as the words came out of her mouth.

"All right," her mother said. "I want to get changed." A few minutes later, she came out of her bedroom wearing a black sweater with rhinestones dotting the sleeves. "You don't even need to change your clothes," her mother said. She put her hand under Harper's chin, her fingertips dry. "Just a little more makeup on your eyes."

•

AT SHORTY'S, THE smell of old beer, soggy wood and cigarettes made Harper sad in the pit of her stomach. A few people sitting at the bar greeted her mother. Behind the bar, a Michelob Light sign had a dark gray gap in its sparkle where something had hit it. Her mother, suddenly jovial, ordered two rum and cokes. The bartender looked at Harper.

"These are both for you, right, Shari?" Hap winked.

She put a bill on the bar. "I'm two-fisted tonight!" She grinned and slid her drinks off the bar, swaying between the tables like a buoy in shallow water. Her mother's deft, expansive mode made her seem like a character in a play. She set the drinks down and pushed one towards Harper.

The drink was sweet and fizzy, with a dark edge, and it tasted surprisingly good. Her mother smiled, conspiratorial, then pushed her chin toward a small platform at the back of the room. "You can do this."

There were only five or six people sitting at small tables; it was pathetic that no one had bothered to come.

The first contestant was a pasty man in a black shirt and jeans. His huge belt buckle, inset with turquoise, highlighted his belly straining at his shirt. He sang a Garth Brooks song and made hand motions like a woman showing merchandise on *The Price is Right*.

"If that's the competition, you can definitely win," her mother said.

Harper's face grew hot. She set down her drink, wove through the tables, and pushed through the louvered doors. A knot of people, laughing and finishing their cigarettes, lingered in the entry, and she felt blocked, claustrophobic, as she pushed past their clumsy bodies. Outside, the night was cool and vaporous. She took a deep breath. Mist rose from the cornfield across the way.

The sound of footsteps in the gravel. Her mother stood in the parking lot, her arms folded across her chest.

"Mom, I'm not going to do it. It's too embarrassing. I don't want a bunch of people staring at me."

"I'm just trying to do something fun with you."

"Great! A little mother-daughter activity. Take your under-age kid to a bar."

Her mother lit a cigarette. "Ease up," she said. Smoke wisped out of her mouth.

"I never even wanted to do it in the first place."

"I thought you wanted to earn some damn money."

"It's cheesy and stupid. I can't just stand up and sing in front of people."

"Well, you can sit out here then, because I've worked my ass off this week, and I deserve to have a night out."

"Have your night!" Harper yelled. Her mother was a shadow, backlit against the lights outside the bar.

"And how are you going to get home?"

"Give me money for a cab."

"I don't have that kind of money."

"If you have money to drink, you have money for a cab. It's only three or four miles."

"You'll have to wait ages for one to come."

"I don't care."

Her mother reached into her pocket, pulled out five dollars, and thrust it at her. "I never thought I'd have a damn daughter who didn't know how to enjoy herself. If you don't have brains, at least you should know how to have a good time." Her mother turned and walked back into the bar.

Harper folded the money and put it in her pocket. She

knew the way home; it was only a few miles. It would take her, probably, an hour to walk, and what else did she have to do?

She'd be five dollars richer. She could call Matt and ask him for a ride—he was probably home, doing something whole-some with his family—but if she called him, saying her mother had left her in the parking lot of a bar, Matt would tell his mother what had happened in order to borrow the car. Harper could imagine his mother gossiping about it in town, on the phone with her country club friends. She set out down the road.

4

AUTUMN'S QUICKENING COOL, the purpose that came with a new school year, gave Harper a feeling of expectancy. If she could take a picture of this scene: the wide field at the side of the school, the low stone wall and trees beyond, it would seem decidedly autumn, although the trees had barely started to turn. It was something to do with the quality of light, the bright finish toward the end of the day.

Janet had stayed after school, too; she'd told her mother she was in the Drama Club to keep her mother from questioning her whereabouts. The ruse seemed comic rather than clever, since Janet so clearly wasn't the drama type. They walked across the playing field and perched on the stone wall at the edge of the school grounds. Janet went on and on about Homecoming, but Harper only half-listened as she counted the weeks backward in her mind. She should have gotten her period by now. She didn't usually pay too much attention when it came, but after the rubber broke, she'd tried to think of when she'd had her last period, the end of July maybe? She'd never gotten it in August, and thought maybe she was just late, and then school started, and there was that whole karaoke thing with her mom, and her period still hadn't come, and she'd tried to put it out of her mind. The bright afternoon, tinged orange, yellow, seemed to press in, grow sharp; Kodachrome, the words from an old song flickered through her mind. The french fries and ketchup she'd had at lunch burned in her throat. A hot fear welled up inside her.

"Hey Janet," she said. "Remember when Nate and Paco were here?"

"Yeah?"

"I might be pregnant."

Janet turned to Harper. Her plastic bluebird barrettes rose on her forehead. "You didn't even tell me you slept with him!"

"Well, I did."

Janet looked off, over the playing field. "Wow . . . I don't mean that you slept with him, but the other thing."

Harper remembered Nate over her, his head against her breasts, the quiet, the sense that they had, in a certain way, met on equal terms. He'd said she would like Olympia, that she would fit there.

"It was good. It was, I don't know. I liked him. And he had a rubber, and then it broke."

"Oh, shit."

"That's what he said."

Janet grinned. Then her expression grew somber.

"I just didn't think I'd get pregnant, or everything else seemed right, I don't know."

"You need to get a home pregnancy test."

"Yeah, Mr. Dimplemeyer works at the Walgreens. That would go over big."

"I'll get you one up in Sandusky. No one will know."

Harper didn't want to bring the test home and leave evidence in the trash, so she took the pregnancy test to the Kwik

Mart, to do it after school. When she walked in the door, the convenience store smell of sour refrigerators, cleanser, and hot dogs turning under heat lamps washed over her. In the bathroom, the linoleum's mottled pattern was obscured by dirt in the corners. A container of bright pink soap, the color of Pepto Bismol, smelled oversweet in the tiny room. She wished there was a better place to do this. She placed paper on the toilet seat, peed into the little cup, then carefully poured it onto the test. Closing her eyes, she waited, her heart thudding. A knock on the door. "Occupied," she called. When the little pink cross came up, she gazed at it, then pressed it to her belly.

•

AUTUMN'S GOLD WAS the color of dying. Harper went to school, did her homework, made sure to be on time for work. She thought of Nate, his loose tangle of hair, his slender torso. What would he think if he knew? Nate, Nathaniel, she didn't even know his last name. Even if she did know it, it was hard to imagine getting in touch with him. What would she say? "Hi, I'm pregnant. Can you believe it?" He was a kid himself. Well, not really. He had just turned twenty-one, but he was solitary, unanchored. Even if she knew Nate's last name, he was gone. Now Harper understood how you could know about something, but didn't truly know until it happened.

•

BY OCTOBER, ALL Harper wanted to do was sleep. She'd missed the bus twice, and her mother had to drive her to school. In class, as the sun shone through the windows, she gazed at bright rectangles on the floor and wished she could curl up in the sun's warmth and sleep. Her mother kept going on about her own senior year, as if it had been the only good time in her life.

Senioritis, she said, when Harper was noticeably tired.

Harper felt as if everything, even thinking, required too

much effort. Part of her wanted to be taken in hand, told what to do, but she was beyond such simplicity. Her friend Katie was the type of girl who had an answer for almost everything, but when Harper told Katie she was pregnant, Katie's lips parted, cheeks flushed; she opened her mouth but nothing came out. She'd finally been presented with a problem that couldn't be solved by pouting or buying something new.

A few days later, Katie insisted on meeting at her house. Katie, with her shining cap of blonde hair, her purposeful lisp, seemed ready for action. Harper wanted to go home and sleep, sleep through the winter, but Katie and Janet had deliberated behind her back, and they insisted that she come.

They met in Katie's bedroom after school. Katie lived in the nice part of town. She had a part-time job at the Motel 6 because her father said he wanted her to learn about the kind of work you had to do if you didn't go to college.

Harper sat, her legs stretched in front of her, on the thick carpet.

Katie closed her bedroom door and locked it. "My brother won't bother us, and my mom is out." She took a deep breath, as if she had prepared a little speech, then sat down in the white painted chair of her desk set. The desk had gold lines edging the drawers, gold-colored drawer pulls. Harper longed to be the kind of girl who would have a desk set in her bedroom.

"Harper," Katie's tone was parental. "I don't know what to tell you, but you seem like you don't believe it, like it will take care of itself, but you know that it won't just go away like that, don't you?"

Harper nodded, moving her open palm in circles over the carpet.

"If you decide to get rid of it, I know where to go in Toledo," Janet said. "They make you do a counseling visit, but my sister went there."

Harper's eyes filled with tears. She'd seen some dumb TV show about how people chose pets with similar traits to their own. Janet would choose a Labrador Retriever, not especially smart, but loyal to the end. Harper wanted to hug her fleshy shoulders.

She couldn't tell them she was afraid of bringing a night that was private and happy, the most true night of her life, out into the open and calling it a mistake. If she decided to have an abortion, which was hard to imagine, she was afraid of the whole official, legal part of it, afraid of revealing herself, of talking to people she didn't know. She'd have to fill out forms, deal with crazy people who might be picketing the clinic. It would all be down in a record that she had done this. Up until now, she had felt that her life was invisible, that she could survive by avoiding detection.

"It's just . . . " Harper tugged on the cuff of Nate's sweatshirt. "I'm scared of the operation."

"Well, if you don't have an abortion, you'll go through a whole pregnancy."

"I know," Harper said. "And that seems impossible, too."

They were all quiet. Harper wished they were sitting around a campfire. She wanted to gaze at something as they contemplated her options.

"My sister said it wasn't so bad," Janet offered. "But she wouldn't do it again."

Harper wanted to tell them that Nate was a happy secret, a key to another world, that having this baby seemed like a link to that world, but when she imagined saying it aloud, she knew it would seem corny and impractical.

"You know, my brother brought the *City Pages* back home last weekend, and I saw an ad from a couple for adoption. I could tell by the area code that they're in Cleveland," Katie said.

Harper looked up, not understanding.

"Harper, I'm telling you, all over the country there are couples who take out ads in places like the *City Pages*. They hope that girls who are pregnant will read the ads and get in touch with them. People are desperate for babies. Since these people are in Cleveland, I bet you wouldn't even have to go anywhere—they'd drive here. Maybe someone who lives near here will adopt it. People who want babies will do anything."

"What if I want to keep it?"

Janet and Katie stared at her. Janet twisted a strand of hair. "How would you manage?" Katie asked.

"I don't know."

"You're always talking about going to college and getting away. How would you get out of here with a baby?"

Harper drew her feet up and sat, cross-legged, on the floor. "Even if I did give the baby up for adoption, if I go through the whole pregnancy, everyone will know."

Katie chewed her lip. "It's true, they will."

"Your mother doesn't know yet, does she?" Janet asked.

Harper shook her head.

"Harper, we'll help you with whatever you want, but you have to decide something—if you just slide along, you won't have any choices," Katie said.

"Do you know how many weeks you are?" Janet asked. "When Nate and Paco were here?"

"It was at the beginning of August. About a week past my birthday." Harper counted from a little past her birthday, August 2. "Six weeks, maybe."

"Do you want to call the people in Cleveland, just to see?" Katie asked.

Harper didn't want to do anything. "Okay," she said. She felt as if someone had opened her chest like a refrigerator door, as if a wind was blowing through her so she couldn't breathe.

Katie pulled the *City Pages* out from under her bed.

They used Janet's cell phone. Harper bent over the ad Katie had circled and punched in the numbers carefully. She wished she was alone.

A woman answered.

"A friend of mine saw your ad in a paper. I, well, I'm seventeen. I've never—. I don't really know what I want to do, but my friend suggested I call you, just to see if you were interested, or ..."

There was a pause. Then the woman said, "Are you trying to say that you're pregnant or that you think you're pregnant?"

"Yes," Harper said. "I'm pregnant." The word was clunky in her mouth.

"And you're trying to figure out what to do?"

"Yes," Harper said. This was backward. She was supposed to be asking the questions but didn't know what to ask. "I don't know if you'd like to meet or something, but there's a Motel 6 close to my house. It's kind of nice. I mean, I don't really know where else I could meet you."

"Where do you live?"

"At home, with my mom."

"I meant, where do you live geographically?"

"Oh," Harper felt stupid. "In Milan, Ohio."

"That's not so far." The woman's voice became more willing. "I didn't know where you were calling from. Sometimes we get calls from Florida, or Alaska, and sometimes ..." She let out a breath. "Last week we flew to Denver, but it turned out to be a joke. Some girls had dared each other to do it. You wouldn't do this as a joke, would you?"

"Oh God, no." Harper imagined a woman getting off a plane with her husband, expectant, finding no one. "That's a shitty thing for someone to do," Harper said. She stopped. She shouldn't have said "shitty" to someone she didn't know.

"Well, we'd like to meet you. You said you're near the Motel 6? I'm guessing there's only one in Milan. My name is Carla Andersson. My husband's name is James. We can get a room there next Friday afternoon, after you're out of school, so we can talk in private."

Katie and Janet sat on the bed, listening to Harper's half of the conversation. The eagerness with which the woman agreed made Harper nervous. "Wait, let me think about my work schedule for a minute," Harper said. Gripping the phone, she mentally went through her Dunkin' Donuts schedule. She started at five on Friday night. "Okay, that works, but I'm not sure of anything. I'm just trying to figure out what to do."

"Of course. We understand."

"The real thing is that you can't call my house or anything. My mother can't know. Not yet."

5

ON THURSDAY NIGHT, Harper washed the dishes, wiped down the counters, scrubbed the stovetop, then told her mother that she wouldn't be home on Friday afternoon. Her mother didn't look up from the television. "Fine," she said.

When Harper walked over to the Motel 6 on Friday afternoon, she took a short cut through the trailer park that occupied a large plot between her apartment complex and the motel. When she was little, before she understood that trailers weren't the sort of thing you aimed to live in, she wanted to see inside them; the rows of homes were child-sized and inviting. David had explained it wasn't like a museum—where anyone was allowed to go. One old woman, with a blue trailer, looked like the Frog from the Frog and Toad books. When Harper said "hello," she croaked "hello" in return. Her mouth was wide and thin, her skin mottled. Harper imagined she could flick out her tongue and capture a fly. Harper had thought it was called a park because everyone was friendly: people visiting between trailers, wash hanging out to dry, flower boxes, kids playing. As she'd grown older, she was careful not to make any friends from there. A thin, blonde girl, Darlene, rode the bus with her, but Darlene was younger, and Harper mostly said "hi" and "bye" to her. She wondered if the Anderssons would think she was from there.

She'd been to the motel before, to meet Katie after work. The Motel 6 was new, with a tiny pool out back. She was reassured by its bright cleanliness.

The clerk at the desk buzzed the couple, then told Harper their room number. Walking down the hall, her heart thudding in her whole body, she felt as if she were on a conveyor belt. She knocked on the door, and the couple answered it together, their outlines filling the doorway. Harper wanted to run. They stepped back, making soothing sounds she didn't understand.

Inside the hotel room, Harper saw the husband was younger than she imagined: a bony-looking man with corn-colored hair combed across his head. His wife was heavy, carefully made-up, with dove-gray eye shadow that matched her outfit. They gestured that Harper should take the armchair. The wife took the desk chair while the husband perched on the bed.

"Thank you so much for calling us," the woman said. "We know this must be hard for you."

Anything Harper might say was swallowed up inside her. She didn't know who should talk first.

"You probably want to know what made us take out an ad —" the husband began.

"We tried fertility treatments, and we tried for quite a while, but they didn't work. The waiting lists for traditional adoptions are very long. . . ." Mrs. Andersson leaned forward in her chair, the flesh from her forearms making furrows where the flesh joined the bone. "We have friends who've been adopted, and one of the problems with traditional adoption is that children, later, seek out their parents, and sometimes it's very difficult. We thought it might be better if a child could have contact with his or her natural parent, that it might be healthier all around."

They waited for her to speak. Harper felt a quivering anxiousness. They seemed like nice people, but she couldn't imagine giving a baby to them. What was wrong with her? How could she keep it? These people were her way out, but somehow, the way didn't seem possible. Jack Sprat and his wife. *Jack Sprat could eat no fat, his wife could eat no lean.* She was afraid she'd spoken the rhyme aloud, but they continued in soft tones, clearly she hadn't. *And so between them both, you see, they licked the platter clean.* The rhyme repeated in her head, obscuring their words. Harper tried to concentrate. Of course they could take care of a baby; they were grown-ups.

"Maybe you could tell us what you're interested in, what you'd like," the woman said.

What could she explain? Suminagashi, the smell of peppermint. Origami swans. Paco making smoothies by peddling a bike? Nate planning to live in a yurt? She didn't want to tell them that making this baby had been easy and happy, with someone who thought she was smart, who believed she didn't belong here.

"I—" Harper looked at the polyester bedcovers, the pictures on the wall that looked like the ones in the McDonald's up the road. "I don't feel like this baby is a mistake. But I don't know what to do about it, either. The real thing is . . . I'm seventeen. I can't raise a baby where I'm living with my mother."

They didn't ask why. She wondered if they could imagine the ashtrays her mother never emptied, the ugly formica, the vomit-colored shag rug in her room, the Payless shoes, the smelly sponge, the contact paper peeling off the cabinets. Could they tell that by looking at her?

The Anderssons talked about playsets, told her they lived in a good school district. He was an accountant. She worked with computer software. They were trying to persuade her without pushing too hard. Everything about them was filled with silent pleading.

"I have to think about this," Harper said. "You seem like nice people. I think I'm going to have the baby, because . . . I don't know, I should do the other thing, but I can't. "

They nodded together, like puppets pulled by the same string. She wasn't used to having the upper hand with an adult, and now she had two grown-ups, watching her for some clue to her feelings, waiting for her decision. All she had to do was promise them a baby. Then she would be free of this huge difficulty. But free to do what? She'd have to finish high school with a GED. Could she even go to college next year? Probably not. Colleges were not going to accept her, certainly not give her a scholarship, with a GED.

"The thing is, you can't call me. My mother doesn't know."

The husband looked as if he wanted to ask something. He moved his jaw as if he had a marble in his mouth.

"Does the father of the baby know about your plans?"

She looked out the window. A man in the trailer park was hanging out laundry, wrestling with a sheet blowing against him. "He doesn't know I'm pregnant. He's a boy I met from out in Washington State. He's kind of a hippie, and . . ." She couldn't admit she didn't know Nate's last name. "It sounds stupid, but he was really nice, and I don't know what he'd say. He doesn't even have a job, and I don't have any way of getting in touch with him. He's living somewhere without a phone or electricity, and . . ." Tears rose in her throat, choking out her words. She couldn't reveal her monstrous stupidity: she had slept with a boy and didn't know his last name. She knew what her mother would say, what everyone would say. Stupid. Dumb. Slut.

The woman got up and came to stand beside her chair. She

patted Harper's back, as if unsure it was all right to touch her. "It's okay, it's okay," she said. "These things happen." The woman stroked her hair and Harper broke into sobs. She wanted to lean into the woman's heavy breasts and weep. They wanted the baby, her baby, which wasn't even real to her, and sitting there, crying, with her face in her hands, she started to cry even harder. She wished they wanted her, that she could start all over again: with a new set of parents, with a mother who wasn't a bitch, with a father who'd stayed. They were being nice because they wanted her baby, not her. Harper felt a sudden anger that they wanted this evidence of her happiness. She sat up, reached for a tissue, and blew her nose.

"I'm sorry, I'm really sorry. I have to think about this."

They gave her their business cards. They wrote their home phones, their cell phones; they told Harper she could call any time.

She imagined they would promise her anything.

6

THE IMMEDIACY OF work was a relief. A wave of high
school kids came in after a swim meet, and their freshly-show-
ered bodies, good-natured jostling, filled her with regret. Some
parents came in to choose donuts for a party, and it was easy to
give them what they wanted: Bismarks filled with cream or jelly, raised or cake, glazed or iced, donut holes or crullers. What
the Anderssons wanted was so much more complicated. She
imagined Mrs. Andersson arriving in a strange airport, looking
out over the waiting area, no one there to meet her.

When little kids came in, Harper saw how they studied the
donuts, how their choices seemed momentous. She explained
what was in the donuts while mothers sipped their coffees,
relieved to have someone else answering questions. Late that
afternoon, a skinny woman pushed through the door with
her wan-looking son, told him he could choose, and the boy
swayed back and forth in front of the cases, sucking on the
string in his windbreaker.

"What's in that one?" he asked Harper.

"Come on," the woman said. "Just choose one."

"What about that one?" He spoke with the string in his mouth; it made a mark on his cheek.

"You can try a different one next time," the woman said.

Harper didn't mind answering his questions; no one else was in line, but the woman finally pointed at the case.

"We'll take one of those," she said.

"That's not the one!" The boy wailed.

"It'll be dinnertime before you choose." The woman leaned down and yanked the string from the boy's mouth. Startled, he put his hands over his lips. His eyes filled with tears.

Harper chose the fanciest looking donut close to where the woman had pointed. She handed it to the boy.

"You'll like this one," she said.

Her kindness didn't penetrate his tears. His mother slapped change on the counter.

Harper understood: it was the choosing that mattered, not the sweet itself.

After they left, Harper made a fresh pot of coffee, then poured out the end of a pot that had been sitting for too long. She didn't want to give Dwight a chance to give her another unnecessary direction; he was always instructing her to take care of something just as she was about to do it. He was like a gnat, buzzing around her. She glanced at the front door, didn't see anyone coming, and decided to restock. As she reached for the stockroom doorknob, the door swung open quickly, almost hitting her in the face. Dwight was breathing as if he'd climbed a hill.

"Oh, Harper, sorry. Are you okay?"

"Yes." She stepped back, then walked over to the shelves to get carry-out coffee lids.

"So Harper, did you grow up around here?" Dwight sounded as if he'd spent a lot of time trying to think up a casual question.

"Sure did." She opened a box of coffee lids, moved to fill the canisters in front, then returned to the back to rip the tape on the box and flatten it for recycling. Dwight was still standing by the shelves.

"I come from a small town myself. This suits me about right," Dwight said.

She stood on her tiptoes to reach for a sleeve of coffee cups. She understood she was supposed to ask where he had grown up, but wished he would just leave her alone.

"Your parents pleased about your job?"

"My mom thinks it's okay."

"Is your Dad here in Milan?"

"No, he lives in Wisconsin."

"That's too bad."

"Not to hear my mother tell it."

He studied her carefully. "We all have our flaws."

"Yes, we do." She opened a box of straws to refill the canisters. She remembered Paco pretending to suck the jelly out of a donut and smiled.

"Why is that funny?"

"What? Oh. No, it's not. I was just thinking of something else."

"I bet your father misses you."

"It'd be nice to think so."

"Why's that?" Dwight looked genuinely curious.

"My mother doesn't talk about it. She says it's better to let sleeping dogs lie."

•

KATIE CALLED FIRST thing the next morning. Harper glanced at her mother's bedroom door then carried the phone into her room.

"So, how was it?"

"Fine, they were nice."

"Do you know what you're going to do?"

"I can't just decide like that," Harper said. What did Katie imagine—that she would decide in an instant, be relieved and grateful, that it would all be fixed? "I had an idea while I was talking to them, though. I could go to the library and get on the Internet and get the phone number of the bike shop in Olympia, Washington. I could call and see if Nate went back to work there." Harper dropped her voice, afraid her mother would hear. "The thing is, can I use your cell phone? I don't want my mom to notice the long distance calls."

"Sure, of course," Katie said.

•

HARPER HAD TO wait for a break in her work schedule to get to the public library after school. The library smelled of varnished wood and paper, wet raincoats and glue—a sheltered, interior smell. Her legs trembled as she sat down in front of the computer. She might be able to find him. She got on Yahoo! and typed in "Olympia Washington Bicycle Shop." There were two, and it struck her that maybe she could get the phone number for the co-op as well.

She met with Katie the next day. Harper pulled a scrap paper of numbers out of her pocket.

"What'd you get?"

"Two bike shops and a co-op."

They went up to Katie's bedroom. "I think it's two hours earlier there," Katie said and closed her bedroom door. Katie had two younger brothers, one of whom Harper never saw. He was like a cat who hid when guests came over. The other brother left Katie and her friends alone. Katie often said there were many benefits to being the only girl in the family, and one benefit was that she had her own room. Harper wished she could be alone now.

She tried the first bike shop. "No, no Nate works here. Try

Karma Cycles. I think he used to work there."

She pushed the numbers for Karma Cycles, and a drawling boy answered the phone. "Nope, he doesn't work here anymore. I think he moved out to the country somewhere."

What could she do? Leave a message? I'm a girl he slept with and I'm pregnant? God, no.

"Well, if you see him, tell him Harper called from Ohio, just to say 'Hi.'"

"What name did you say? Harper? Okay, cool."

Harper knew he'd forget, as soon as he hung up. She tried the co-op.

"You want to speak to Nate? Do you know what department he works in?"

"No, I don't."

"I think there's a new guy in produce."

Her chest thudded. The line clicked as the girl transferred her. A voice with a British accent answered.

"Is this Nate?" Harper asked.

"Yes, it is."

"I'm sorry," she said. "I'm looking for another Nate. I must have the wrong number." Harper would always associate these phone calls with Katie's yellow and white bedroom, the crisp eyelet coverlet, the desk set that matched her headboard. What would Nate think if he knew? She guessed that, even if he wasn't ready or willing to raise a baby, he would still want to know, he'd try to help somehow. He'd say, "Come live in the yurt!" He would be helpful and kind; he would want her around. She glanced at the pile of magazines lying in the corner.

Headlines about purses, shoes, fall colors, how to get rid of acne. He loves me, he loves me not.

Maybe she was wrong about Nate. She wished she knew.

•

WHEN HARPER COULDN'T snap her jeans, she felt frightened. Her waist thickened, her breasts grew larger—her whole shape was becoming unfamiliar. She had always been small. This new heaviness felt as if she were becoming un-like herself. She didn't want to ask her mother for money for clothes and didn't want to spend any of her own—her bank account was her saving for escape. One afternoon, she mailed David a withdrawal slip and asked him to sign it for her.

She said it was for Christmas presents.

As the weather grew colder, Harper wore Nate's Evergreen sweatshirt almost every day, hoping it would hide her thicken-ing form.

"All those donuts are starting to get to you," her mother said one night. "Nothing but fat and sugar. You don't want to get the Metzer butt." She lit a cigarette and studied Harper.

Harper picked up her mother's dinner plate and carried it, with her own, to the sink. She couldn't look her mother in the eye.

"So, where are you applying?"

Harper sighed. "Ohio State, Bowling Green, Kent State. There's application fees, so I can't apply all over the place." Even a few weeks ago, the question would have made her happy. Harper wondered if her mother's question was a dig, if her mother knew.

•

LATER THAT WEEK, after school, Matt stopped in front of her locker. His short brown hair, freshly cut, made him seem younger. He rubbed his ear. They'd hardly talked since school started.

"I've been really busy with football practice and application essays," he said. On his thumb, he'd bitten the cuticle and skin all down one side; the skin was pink and torn.

"I know. Me, too." Harper said. "Not with football, though."

He started to ask a question, then fiddled with something on his pack. "Are we broken up?" Matt asked.

"I have a job after school now."

"You don't have to pretend," he said. "Let's talk outside."

She gathered her books and walked out the side door with him. Wood smoke and autumn damp wafted through the air. He leaned into the wind. Something in him had turned outward.

"I applied early decision to Dartmouth. I don't know if I'll get in. Did you apply out of state?"

"I can't afford to."

She guessed he wanted to go out with someone else. His gratitude had evaporated. "Matt?"

"Yeah?"

"You're a free agent. You can ask out whoever you want."

"Okay, then." And he turned and walked toward the bus.

7

FOR AN EARLY Christmas present, Katie gave her an oversized Guatemalan sweater. "This will hide anything," she giggled. "Actually, I kind of like it, but if anyone asks why you're wearing such a hairy thing, you can say my feelings will be hurt if you don't wear it."

Harper smiled, grateful for Katie's practicality; she sensed that Katie was saving up something in her accounting. If Katie's parents gave her a hard time about anything, she would always be able to point to Harper and say, "Well, at least I didn't do that."

Dwight had decorated the Dunkin' Donuts with Christmas lights, although he'd stewed over a corporate memo saying that all decorations were supposed to be "holiday" decorations, and therefore non-denominational. Yesterday, she had barely gotten her coat off when he came up and stood at her elbow.

"Did you hear what happened at church?"

"No, what?"

"Some kids stole the baby Jesus out of the nativity scene."

"That's not right."

"We don't have a spare, so I don't know what we'll do."
Dwight worked his mouth from side to side.

It was like talking to a two-year-old. If the people at his
church couldn't figure out how to buy a doll, they must be a
pretty pathetic lot. She wished Dwight would just let her do
her job. It was strange to have someone stupid in charge.

At the end of her shift, moving through the kitchen,
Harper knocked a container of sprinkles off the counter. The
brittle plastic broke and scattered red and green sprinkles all
over the floor. Cursing under her breath, she got a broom and
dustpan. Christmas sucked. If David came home, which was
the only thing that could make Christmas bearable, he would
take one look at her and know. If he didn't come home, she'd be
alone with her mother. She wasn't sure which was worse.

She used to daydream that one day her father would come
to his senses and realize he had a daughter who, in spite of his
absence, had grown up to be worth noticing. He'd say, "You're
lovely! Why didn't I know? I've missed so much time with you."
She had played this scene in her head so many times that, once
set in motion, it ran its own course. Now, her imagining was
too much at odds with reality. If her father met her, what would
he say? "So, you got yourself knocked up. Good work, kid."

His birthday card had arrived three weeks late with a little
note inside. *Happy Birthday. Sorry this is so late. Buy yourself
something pretty.* A folded $20 bill, its corner torn, inside. The
envelope had a return address in La Crosse, Wisconsin. She
didn't mention it to her mother, but tucked the money away.

Harper pulled on a pair of mittens and stepped outside
to walk to work. Snow sprinkled the parking lot outside the
apartment, and the thin layer of white made everything look
clean. It wouldn't last until Christmas, but the swirling flakes
in the gray sky, a patternless swirling, soothed her. She trudged
up the side of the road. The ground had frozen in awkward

clumps; the sound of traffic was muted. When she pushed open the front door, the smell of sugar made her want to be outside again. In back, she pulled her bulky sweater off, over her head, to put on her Dunkin' Donuts apron. She jumped when she realized that Dwight had come into the room. He looked down at her stomach and recognition blossomed on his face.

"Come into my office."

Harper followed.

He closed the door. "I wondered if it was the donuts, or something else, but clearly, it's something else. We absolutely cannot have an unmarried pregnant woman working for our company."

"But I'm engaged!"

He stared at her, then touched the edge of his desk with both hands, as if connecting to some power that would both ground and enlighten him.

"My boyfriend, Matt, and I are engaged. We're going to tell our families at Christmas; that's why I haven't been wearing a ring." Harper looked him in the eye.

"Well," Dwight was caught off-guard. "You haven't mentioned this young man to me before."

"It's not the kind of thing I discuss at work." Harper pursed her lips, tried to sound prissy.

Dwight worked his mouth. God, he was stupid, Harper thought.

•

AT HOME THAT night, Harper made sure the apartment was empty before calling Katie. "Katie, listen, my boss knows. He saw me getting changed."

"What!"

"Not like that. I was taking off my sweater to put on my apron. I can't believe this, but I told him I was engaged."

"Wow," Katie giggled. "Did he believe you?"

"I don't know, but what can he say? The thing is, I need a ring. Do you have one I can borrow? It can be cheap, it doesn't matter. Just something I can take on and off. . . ."

"Let me look . . ."

Harper heard her rustling around her room. Then Katie came back to the phone.

"I bet my mother has an old ring she doesn't wear."

"I don't want to borrow one of your mother's rings."

"Well, I can look more later."

Katie took a deep, preparatory breath, and Harper knew what was coming. "Harper, did you think about those people who want to adopt the baby?"

"Yeah, I did. A lot. Katie, the thing is, they were really nice and all, but they seemed, I don't know, like aliens. Not like outerspace, but I can't imagine having a baby and just handing it over to them."

Katie was silent, and Harper sensed her disappointment. She knew that Katie wanted to find a solution.

"The thing is, I still don't know what I'm going to do. My mother'll go nuts when she figures it out."

"I bet."

Harper heard her mother's key in the lock. "I have to go! I'll talk to you tomorrow." Harper hung up the phone and hurried to her room to change. She wore sweatpants at home when her mother was around, but if dopey Dwight could see she was pregnant, it was just a matter of time before her mother figured it out.

When the phone rang again, Harper hurried to answer it. Her mother was drinking a beer, watching the news, and she looked up to see if it was for her. Harper mouthed "David" and her mother smiled and nodded, indicating Harper should talk to him.

"Hey there," David said. "I got a ride from a friend, so I'm coming for a few days. Don't think I can take much more."

"It'll be great to see you," she said.

"What's wrong?"

"We'll talk when you get here," Harper said.

•

THE DAY BEFORE Christmas, Harper pulled on her fuzzy bathrobe and walked into the kitchen, where her mother was sipping coffee.

"I only work a half-day today," her mother said. "I'll probably stop for groceries on the way home. Shopping might take a while."

Harper nodded. Her mother was trying to do things right, which meant cooking a holiday-like meal, and at least getting drunk at home. When David lived at home, they'd pretended to be a semi-normal family, but with David gone, her mother stopped pretending. She didn't go to open house nights at school; she signed Harper's report cards without looking at them. Harper had thought of David like a mountain climber, climbing ahead of her, holding a rope that would guide her and keep her from falling. She didn't know what would happen now.

When her mother left, Harper opened the windows in spite of the cold and vacuumed the whole apartment. She cleaned methodically, knowing that everything would look better when she was done.

•

A COLD RAIN made the day seem darker than it was. When her mother came home, she carried the grocery bags up the steps and set them inside the door. Her boots made gray puddles on the linoleum Harper had just cleaned. Harper put an old towel by the front door, then ferried the bags from the doorway into the kitchen. The box from the liquor store was too heavy, and she left it by the door.

From the doorway, Harper saw a car pull up in the parking lot, and the outline of David, carrying a duffle bag, getting out of the passenger side. Harper hurried into the kitchen with the last grocery bag. She heard his footsteps, his deep voice, her mother greeting him.

"Hi, sweetheart. Look at you! You're still growing, I can hardly believe it." Harper kept putting food in the cabinet.

"Where's Harper?"

"Here I am," she called, and walked into the hall.

When David looked at her, the grin faded from his face. She looked back, willing him to hide his reaction, to move past his first thought, to his second, but he just looked.

"Jeezus."

"David, please."

David looked at his mother, who was watching him closely, and then she turned to study Harper. Realization settled over her face.

"Some fucking donut. I did wonder, but I tried to give you the benefit of the doubt. What a stupid kid you are."

"What the hell did you do?" David looked stunned.

"What do you think I did?" Harper turned and walked into her room, closing the door behind her.

She could hear them in the living room, her mother shouting so Harper would hear. "How stupid! Stupid fucking bitch. At least I graduated from high school!"

Then David's voice, hard and low. She couldn't make out the words, but a counterbalance to his mother.

She locked her bedroom door. Through the wall, she heard them pour themselves drinks, settle in, turn on the TV. An hour or so later, when Harper had to use the bathroom, her mother looked up from the television.

"Please tell me it was Matt that knocked you up, so we can get something from those snotty parents of his."

"It wasn't Matt," she said.

"Who?"

"He's not from around here."

"Oh, great!" her mother said. "Does he know? Does he care?"

Her mother's eyes were red, her short hair in disarray. Christmas lights, from outside the building, flashed red and green on her cheek. Harper had to keep her mother separate from that night. Saying Nate had just been in town for a few days, describing a night in the back of a truck, would sound ugly and cheap. She wished she could summon up that peace and stillness and early morning warmth, but it seemed so far away now.

"You do know who the father is, don't you?"

"Of course."

"Don't get snotty with me. How far along are you?"

"Four and a half months."

"Good Christ." Her mother slammed her glass down on the table. "Why didn't you say something sooner? You could have done something about it."

"I thought you wanted to get out of here," David said.

"I did, I do. A rubber broke."

David threw up his hands in a gesture of exasperation, then went to the kitchen to get another beer.

•

ON CHRISTMAS MORNING the pale, cloud-covered sky looked like lead. She felt as if she hadn't moved all night. A soft knock on her door.

"Who is it?"

"It's me. Can I come in?"

Harper didn't answer, but David came into the room and sat down on her bed. His hair had grown shaggy, the blond a shade darker. He ran his hand through it, then looked down at her school notebooks, as if he couldn't look her in the eye.

"Why didn't you have an abortion?"

"I didn't want to."

"Why not?"

She wanted to say that it had seemed too public, too exposing, but by now she knew her reasoning was silly. There was nothing more public and exposing than what she was going through, but it was too late to do anything about it now. "I've thought of giving it up for adoption."

"Well, you should. You can't stay here with Mom and a baby. You'll go crazy."

"I know."

"I'm sorry I was mean, but Harper, it was a stupid thing to do. You should have gotten rid of it while you could."

"I know you're right, but I didn't want to."

David rubbed his open hand over his face. Even hungover, he was handsome. "You might as well get up and get dressed. I'm going to make some Bloody Marys. Maybe Mom will mellow out."

Harper lay still when he left the room. She'd made the wrong decision. She should have gotten rid of it. She'd thought only in terms of hiding it, or sheltering a memory; she didn't think of the baby as an actual person. Everything felt different now that it was out in the open. Now, she had to think about money and going to a doctor. On the day she went to the library, she'd wanted to look at the books about pregnancy. *What to Expect When You're Expecting* was right on the shelf, but if anyone saw what she was reading, they'd know. Besides, she felt fine. She didn't feel nauseous, except around her mother's smoke. She was more aware of how everything smelled now: car exhaust, perfume, old coffee. Whenever her mother went out, Harper opened the windows to get some fresh air.

She rolled onto her other side. How would she get through

this day, this pregnancy, life after that? It seemed impossible.

•

THE FOLLOWING DAY, Harper came into the kitchen, where David and her mother were both drinking coffee. He had bought their mother a coffee maker for Christmas, joking that it was time for her to stop drinking Taster's Choice. Harper wanted to bring up the subject of the doctor before he left town; she hoped her mother would be more reasonable if David was there.

"Mom, I think I should go to the doctor, just for a check-up."

"Sure," her mother said. "Fat lot of good a check-up is going to do you now."

"Should I make an appointment with Dr. Snyder?"

"God, you are stupid. He's a pediatrician, and the state you're in is not for kids. You should call the practice and say you want an appointment with the OB/GYN."

"I can go by myself," Harper said.

"Damn right you will. I'm not taking time off to drag you to the doctor."

David opened his mouth and looked at their mother as if he might say something. Then he poured himself another cup of coffee.

8

ON THE AFTERNOON of her doctor's appointment, the air was crystalline, the sun bright, every tree branch sharp against the sky.

Walking into the clinic, its warmth, its antiseptic smell and benign indifference were a relief. A nurse weighed her and took her blood pressure. Harper had never been to a grown-up doctor before. Janet and Katie's mothers had taken them to a gynecologist, and they'd told Harper about how you had to lie on a table, about the stirrups, about how weird and uncomfortable the whole thing was.

When she got out of her warm clothes, Harper felt cold and ridiculous wearing a paper gown. Posted around the room were cross-section pictures of a baby inside a woman, all in different stages. The early pictures of outsized heads and nubbin limbs made her think of elementary school, when they'd planted lima beans in plastic cups lined with moist paper towels. The pictures, pastel and foreign, felt unrelated to what was happening inside her.

When the doctor came into the room, chart in hand, he

looked at Harper, then set the chart down on the table. Dr. Watkins' stomach bulged under his white coat. Almost completely bald, a fringe of dark hair rimmed the back of his head. With his wide face and gold-rimmed glasses, everything about him seemed round.

"Hello, Harper. I'm Doctor Watkins." When he shook her hand, his grasp was warm.

His smile seemed genuine, and he didn't appear horrified or angry. "Let's talk for a few minutes before I examine you." He sat down in a chair looked down at her chart. "So you're pregnant, and this is your first visit."

She nodded.

"And you're well into your second trimester."

"My mother is really angry. She said I should have had an abortion." As soon as she spoke, Harper realized it was too blunt. He hadn't asked about her mother.

He looked down at her chart, made a mark. "Those kind of decisions are really up to you. What are your plans after the baby is born?"

Harper reached for her wrist, wanting to twist the fabric of her cuff, but there was nothing to hold on to.

"I met some nice people, who want to do an open adoption. Everyone tells me that people with money can do more for a child, and I know that's right, but I told the people I couldn't promise."

He studied her for a long moment before speaking. "As a doctor—legally, ethically—it would be wrong for me to sway you one way or another, but if you're going to have the baby, you have plenty of time to decide. The decision really is up to you."

Harper took a deep breath. "The thing is, it should seem like a relief, I mean, the idea that I could give it up. But when I imagine giving a baby away . . ." She looked at the wall with its signs and posters, the typed explanations. "All I see is white. Like I can't imagine what's in front of me. People act like, if I gave the baby up, that it would be like it never happened, and I could just get on with my life. But it would never be like it didn't happen. I would always know. And the baby would always know. I don't like my mother very much, but at least she had me, she kept me, even if she's kind of a bitch." Harper stopped, embarrassed that she'd let this slip. "I mean, I think I'd feel worse if she'd given me away."

It felt strange to be saying so much, but things that seemed confusing when they were inside her head somehow became clear when she said them aloud. She would feel worse if her mother had given her up. David would be out in the world, and they wouldn't even know about each other.

"And the father of the baby?"

"He's a boy I met. He lives in Washington State."

"That's not what I meant. Does he know?"

She shook her head.

"Well, you also have to think of the legal implications. You can't sign off on an adoption without his consent."

Harper felt a strange, almost physical tug in her gut. She couldn't give the baby up without telling Nate. She was quiet for a moment, trying to think. The law was an odd stroke of luck, a kind of protection.

"What if I can't find him?"

"I'm not sure how it all works. If you do decide to give up the baby, we refer you to Social Services, and they work on the legal aspects of this."

"I'm not sure that's what I want to do anyway."

"Well, let's examine you and see how you're doing."

"My mom said we shouldn't do anything that costs extra."

He turned toward a drawer and opened it. Harper felt a heat in her throat, a combination of anger and shame.

He listened to her heart, had her breathe in, breathe out. He checked her pulse. "Do you want to hear the baby's heartbeat?"

"Can I?"

"Sometimes it's hard to hear. It depends where the baby is. Let me find it first." He placed the earpieces of his stethoscope in his ears, the chrome disc on her belly. He moved it around, listening. His round cheek was freshly shaven, his scalp shiny. She could tell he didn't hear anything, and suddenly, she was frightened. What if something was wrong? He stopped, listening carefully. He held the stethoscope on the right side of her belly.

"Okay now." He took the stethoscope out of his ears and handed it to her. "It won't sound like what you imagine a heartbeat is. It's much faster."

She placed the stethoscope in her ears, and he slowly moved the disc around the same place on her belly. He paused, looking at Harper for some sign she could hear it, but she didn't hear anything at all.

Then she heard a fast, liquid, whooshing sound. She looked up at him, felt herself grinning, and nodded. *Whish, whish, whish, whish, Whish, whish, whish, whish* . . . So fast! So tiny! Like the heartbeat of a bird. She couldn't believe it. *Whish, whish, whish, whish, Whish, whish, whish, whish.* "That quick sound? That's a heartbeat?"

"Yes, it is."

"I want to keep hearing it."

He nodded that she should put the stethoscope back in her ears. She did, but the sound had faded. She looked up at him and said, "I can't hear it so well now."

He moved the stethoscope down a bit.

"There," she said. *Whish, whish, whish, whish, Whish, whish, whish, whish. Whish, whish, whish, whish.* Utterly still, she listened. She never would have imagined a baby's heartbeat could be so liquid, fluttering, not imagined it like this.

Finally, she took the stethoscope off her ears and looked up. "That's amazing," she said.

"I'd like to do a sonogram," Dr. Watkins said.

"Does it cost extra?"

"Don't worry about that right now. Would you like to know whether it's a boy or a girl?"

She nodded.

They moved to an adjoining room, where a nurse put cold, transparent gel on her belly.

Harper focused on the monitor. The odd curves, the black and white lines, didn't look like a baby inside her.

Dr. Watkins studied it carefully. "Well, everything looks good. We can never say for sure, but I think you're going to have a little girl."

Harper smiled and felt an unreasonable happiness welling up inside her; she didn't think to call it joy.

9

HARPER HAD ALWAYS avoided drawing attention to
herself. At school, she and Katie and Janet had been their own
little group, neither popular nor unpopular, and so did not
invite attention. Going to the prom with Matt had made her
register briefly, but now that she was showing, people would
talk. She'd be logged in the annals of Thomas Edison High:
Harper Canaday, the Girl Who Got Pregnant Senior Year.
Everyone would remember. The first day back, after Christmas,
she stood at her locker, taking off her hat and mittens. Janet's
locker was next to hers, and when Harper took off her coat,
Janet looked down at her stomach.

"It's because you're so little," Janet said. "If it was me, being
such a tub, no one would notice." Together they walked into
homeroom and sat down in back. In the loud buzz of conversation, with everyone comparing notes about Christmas vacation,
no one seemed to notice her.

Between classes, Harper held her books in front of her and
hurried down the hall, trying to get to class early so she could
sit in back. A few people glanced her way, but she didn't want

to see if anyone really noticed.

At lunchtime, she'd have to wait in line for milk then walk across the cafeteria. As she stepped across the open room, through the clatter of noise and laughter bouncing off the glazed brick walls, Harper felt it grow quiet around her.

Paul Prentiss, the class joker, called out, "Packing it on there, Harper, huh?" Harper stared at the bricks above his head and tried to smile at his offhand tone. Her face grew hot; the sound around her dimmed. A wave of embarrassment rolled up behind him. From the faces around him, the expressions of surprise, she saw he'd merely meant to tease her about her weight, and hadn't fully realized what he'd touched on.

The walls of the lunchroom swayed around her; she gripped her tray.

"Harper, over here!" Katie called, and Harper walked toward her familiar voice.

•

IN THE LUNCHROOM, in classes, Katie and Janet surrounded her, but when she walked across the lunchroom or down the hall, Harper felt the gazes of those around her. When Matt saw her, later that afternoon, the fear on his face was transparent. She'd slept with him only once, in June. He stared at her, at her stomach, then turned away.

The following morning, he came up to her locker. Janet gave Harper a steadying look, then closed her locker and walked down the hall toward homeroom. People around them grew quiet, as if pretending not to listen. Matt's pallor made the downy hairs on his lip stand out. He rubbed his eyes; the skin around his thumb was torn and bleeding.

"You're pregnant?"

"Yes."

"It's not mine—is it?"

"No, it's not."

He gazed at her in wonder, as if trying to make out her features underwater. Then his face grew square, his chin firm. "I can't believe you. I thought you, of anyone, would get out of here."

"I will."

"Not like that you won't."

She raised her eyebrows.

"My mother was right about you," Matt said. "The fruit doesn't fall far from the tree."

She felt hot, as if she'd been struck. She opened her mouth to speak, but didn't know what to say, and so bent down, pretending to look for something in her locker. Matt's footsteps moved away, down the hall. When she straightened up, she wanted to call his name, but he had moved off into the crowd. The students in the hall turned back to their lockers.

Today, she had to tell the gym teacher why she was dropping of out of PE. Harper wished she could avoid the conversation, but she couldn't get changed with everyone else. Before fourth period, Harper hurried to talk to her while the other girls were changing. Ms. Perkins' office was a tiny cinderblock room that was more like a broom closet than an office. Harper knocked on her door, and Ms. Perkins looked up from the paperwork on her desk.

"Come in, have a seat."

"Can I close the door?"

Ms. Perkins raised her eyebrows above her glasses. "You can, if you want to move that stuff—" She pointed to a plastic crate of papers. "But it gets claustrophobic in here. Why don't you leave it open a little, just for air?"

Harper pulled the crate into the room and closed the door, sealing them in a cinderblock tomb.

"I'm pregnant," Harper said. It felt strange to say it aloud. "I don't think I can take PE anymore."

"That's a shame," Ms. Perkins said, and Harper knew she

didn't mean only about class. "You know, you can't drop out of PE altogether. Some exercise is healthy for you—you can walk around the track as the weather gets warmer, but we need to schedule a meeting with the school counselor to discuss your situation."

Fear crept over her. She didn't want to discuss this with strangers.

"Since you're required by law to go to school until you turn eighteen, you can't simply decide that you're done with school because you're pregnant. When is your baby due?"

"In the middle of May."

"Do you think you could still finish? Get some of your work done early?"

"I probably could. I mean, school's pretty easy."

"Well, we'll make an appointment with Mrs. Livingston. We strongly encourage students to stay in school. If you want drop out, it becomes a legal matter, and you have to submit a study plan, which your parents, your teachers, and the principal will sign off on. There are a few other procedures, too. I don't know the whole drill."

"I thought I'd just stop coming when I got too pregnant. I thought that's what people did."

Mrs. Perkins raised one side of her mouth, as if trying to smile. "Harper, that might have been the case years ago, but nobody pretends this doesn't happen anymore. We don't want a young woman to drop out and drift without skills. In the state's eyes, it's an economic matter. If we let pregnant young women just drop out of school, we end up with more unedu- cated women on welfare. Your parents may not be too happy with you right now, but here at school, and hopefully with any medical treatment you get, we're not here to pass judgment on your behavior. You're pregnant. It's done. So now it's a matter of trying to have a healthy baby, and then figuring out what your options are." She picked up a basketball resting on a crate and bounced it on the floor; the slap echoed off the walls of the tiny room. "Believe me, you're not the first girl this has happened to. Not by a long shot."

•

THE JANUARY AFTERNOON was gray and raw, and Harper was glad to get home. She wanted to get away from school and absorb these ideas that seemed so normal for everyone else. She'd imagined that, given her humiliation, the stupidity of the whole thing, she'd just drop out of school when she got too big, and everyone would leave her alone. The prospect of coming up with a formal plan of study, meeting with the principal, bringing her mother to meetings—all seemed impossible. She'd thought that she could retreat, and the price of that retreat would be loneliness and boredom. It was strange to realize that there would be no escape.

She closed the front door, grateful for the apartment's quiet. Hidden in a box under her bed were the Andersson's business cards. They'd be at work, but she couldn't call in the evening, when her mother might come home. What could she to say to them? Are you still interested? She thought of Dr. Watkins, how kind he'd been.

What did she want? She wanted to get away from her mother, get out of Milan, but she didn't know how to do it with a baby. Just getting through her pregnancy seemed like a long time.

She picked up the phone and dialed Mrs. Andersson at work. Harper expected a secretary to answer, and so was startled when Mrs. Andersson picked up.

"Hi, this is Harper. I met you in Milan?"

"Oh, hello." Mrs. Andersson sounded surprised, and Harper imagined her mentally refocusing, trying to shift gears. "How are you?"

"I'm okay." Harper felt her voice crack. "Actually, I'm not

okay. Everyone knows I'm pregnant now, and it's kind of weird." She took a deep, trembling breath. "I just wanted to say that I went to the doctor, and everything looks fine, but everything's strange, and I just don't know what to do."

"Harper, I know this is hard. I'm glad you called to let me know."

"You seem like really nice people." Harper's voice broke. She tried to catch her breath. "The doctor thinks it's a girl."

"A little girl?" The woman's voice softened.

"I know it's not right for me to call you like this, but there's no one else I can talk to."

"Was the doctor nice?"

"Yes," Harper gulped. "He was."

"Harper, while you're deciding, if there's anything else you want—if you want to meet with us again, see our house, anything like that—all you have to do is call."

"Okay," Harper said. "Good-bye."

She hung up the phone. The air around her, gray and particular, made everything seem too real. She wanted to cry, but it wouldn't provide any release. Harper wished the Anderssons would take her and the baby. Maybe she could have two parents, start all over again. They would treat Harper like a daughter, the baby like her younger sister. Two for one, a package deal. Harper started to weep. Her idea was ridiculous—they wanted a baby, the way people wanted kittens rather than a half-grown cat. And she was supposed to be grown up now. Harper put her face in her pillow. She couldn't just do her childhood over again to make it right. She reminded herself that Mrs. Andersson sounded kind because she had to be nice—they wanted her baby. Harper felt a sick guilt in her stomach. It was wrong for her to call them, to need them, but she felt pulled toward kindness like an animal seeking warmth.

•

HER MOTHER CAME home, pulling in a cloud of smoke and cold air. After announcing she'd make dinner, she plopped into the recliner and started punching numbers into the phone. Harper lay on the couch, watching commercials for upcoming shows—all of them about crime.

"Who were you calling in Cleveland?" her mother asked. Harper hit MUTE.

"I can call the number myself and find out," her mother said.

She didn't want her mother to talk to the Anderssons. She didn't trust her not to do something weird or desperate. Harper had seen shows like *Law and Order*, she knew that people couldn't buy babies, but she could imagine her mother trying to negotiate: making her give up the baby for a year's tuition at school, a downpayment on a car.

"Some people."

"Don't be a smartass."

"I was talking to people about adoption."

"Good." Her mother rose to get herself a drink.

Harper moved past her, poured a glass of milk, took some chocolate chip cookies, and went to her room. Dinner would probably be a while. If she offered to cook, her mother would get pissed, yell that Harper was implying she was too drunk to feed them properly. It would be easier to wait. Harper had read everything Dr. Watkins had given her about nutrition and felt his approval when she answered his questions: "No, I don't smoke. No, I don't drink. No, I don't do any drugs." None of that had really mattered before. Mainly, she didn't do those things because she didn't want to be like her mother, but now it was good for another reason, and this pleased her.

She ate the milk and cookies and lay on her back in bed. When she imagined giving the baby up, the future seemed like the white buzzing of the TV when all the shows were over, an electronic blizzard. She couldn't see ahead. She flipped through *Seventeen*, then tossed it on the floor. Something pushed in her stomach, below her right breast. She sat up a little, wondering if something was wrong. She felt it again, a tiny push. The baby was kicking! It didn't feel like a kick at all. She pulled up her shirt. Her belly was bigger now, and she looked for some external sign, but couldn't see anything. She kept very still, and felt it again, a determined little nudge. A baby girl swimming inside her. She rested her hand on her belly.

10

HER MOTHER STARTED coming home more often, making dinner, which Harper wanted to take as a sign of concern, but didn't quite trust. Harper could imagine her at happy hour, slapping her money down on the bar. "Yeah, my daughter went and got herself knocked up. Guess I should get home and make her dinner." She'd play the role of a martyr.

One night, her mother came home and made hamburgers. The meat smelled wonderful and, as soon as her mother put their plates on the table, Harper poured ketchup on her burger and took a huge bite.

"So, what are these people like?" Her mother made it sound as if a previous conversation had been interrupted by something inconsequential.

"They're nice. They want to do an open adoption."

"Which means?"

"That the baby would be able to know me."

"But it would be a secret that you're the mother?"

"I'm not sure."

"What would it call you?"

"I don't know."

"What if something's wrong with the baby? Would they still want it?"

The meat in Harper's mouth suddenly felt gummy and hard. It hadn't crossed her mind that something could be wrong. She had only imagined a happy, sweet, pink baby. Her mother lit a cigarette, her lips puckering, and Harper felt her mother's poison, always spreading doubt and fear.

"People want white babies who are healthy."

"And your point is—"

Her mother took a bite of hamburger and stared at her.

"The baby's father is white, if that's what you're asking."

"Can he interfere, legally?"

Harper looked down at her plate, then wiped the corners of her mouth. "I'd have to find him. He'd have to sign off on it."

"He's not married, is he?"

"No!" Harper was shocked. "He's a teenager, like me."

Her mother's eyes narrowed.

"He's not from around here," Harper said.

"Well, you should track him down, because he owes you," her mother said.

Lying in bed that night, Harper imagined Mrs. Andersson's neatly made up face, her jowls, her gray eye shadow. Mr. Andersson had faded in her memory, although she remembered his bright yellow hair. Harper knew it was cruel to keep them hoping, but she still wasn't sure what to do. People kept telling her how hard it would be to keep the baby. You have no idea, they said. She imagined herself working in a little shop. A woman in town, who owned an antiques store, kept her baby with her in an old-fashioned cradle. She rocked the baby and fed it right there in the shop. Harper hoped she could get a job like that.

•

AT WORK, HARPER wore a cubic zirconia ring that Janet had borrowed from her older sister. Harper never wore it at school—no one would be fooled. Dwight was less interested in talking to her these days. He stayed in his office, doing paperwork, or supervised whoever was making donuts. A few regular customers asked when she was due, and when Dwight was in earshot, their questions made her flinch.

"My doctor says mid-May, but my fiancé thinks it'll be sooner." Harper tried to imitate the fond, confiding tone she heard other women use. The word *fiancé* felt awkward on her tongue.

She had saved $563. 96. More money than she'd ever had in her life. People kept saying she couldn't work and have a baby. Didn't women in Africa and Asia strap babies to their backs and work in the fields? She imagined a sleeping baby tucked against her back.

•

THE WEATHER BROKE: ice melting to slush, the wind of coming warmth, but instead of feeling energized, as everyone else seemed to, Harper felt tired and wrung out. The store smelled oversweet, the scent of coffee unappealing. She put on her apron, which by now looked ridiculous over her stomach. Three junior girls giggled at the end of the counter, but they stopped when they saw her and returned to their huddle.

Before she went out front, Dwight called her into his office. On the wall behind his desk was a new bulletin board, plastered with family photos, as if the board was meant to illustrate a better way of life. Dwight sat down behind his desk and gestured that she should take a seat.

"Harper, I've come to understand that you're not engaged at all—that this was a deliberate lie you told to keep this job." Dwight lowered his voice. "You cannot work here any longer. And you are not to take any company property with you, so please make sure you leave your apron behind."

Harper stared at a piece of donut stuck between his teeth. Oh! as if she actually wanted to take an apron with her! She thought for a minute; she had a paycheck coming. She narrowed her eyes, tried not to look at his mouth.

"I received something for you a few days ago. We are not a post office here. This must be from one of your many admirers." He handed her a postcard with a picture of water and pine trees. It was addressed: Harper, Dunkin Donuts, Rte 523, Milan, Ohio. The neat, narrow handwriting was a boy's.

Harper—

Winter in the yurt was pretty damp. I'm thinking heat, at least a woodstove, might be good in the future. Spring is coming to Olympia, and I hope it's there as well. I still think you'd like it here.

Nate

She flushed and looked up at Dwight, who was staring at her, waiting for her to leave. "I'll expect my final paycheck," she said.

"The bookkeeper has already taken you off direct deposit. She'll probably mail it to your home address."

"I'll be waiting for it."

"We'll get it to you when we have time," Dwight said.

Holding the postcard in her hand, Harper trembled with anger. She couldn't believe Dwight had kept it from her. She deserved her paycheck, too.

"If you try to screw me out of it, I'll call your wife and tell her about you jerking off in the stock room," Harper said. She used the arms of the chair to push herself up, then walked out of his office, slamming the door behind her.

11

AT HOME, HARPER sat in her bedroom, running her fingers over the lines of blue ink, as if the card was a magic lamp and Nate might appear before her. The blurry postmark didn't reveal when he'd sent the card. Had they been thinking of each other at the same time? *I still think you'd like it here.*

She picked up the phone to call Janet. "Oh, you won't believe this," Harper said. "I got a postcard from Nate."

"That's great."

"What's wrong?"

"Nothing's wrong. I just worry for you. How did he know where to send it?"

"He sent it to Dunkin' Donuts. Dwight wasn't even going to give it to me, but I guess he decided to clean house." Harper stopped, set the postcard down, and stared at the picture as if wishing she could step into it. "I saw some girls from school there. Someone must have told Dwight I wasn't really engaged."

"He fired you?"

"Yeah." Harper lay down on her bed, still holding the

phone. "I guessed it was just a matter of time, but I'm bummed. I need the money."

"Was Nate's last name on the postcard?"

"No." Harper traced his name with her finger.

"I have to go," Janet said. "My mom's pissed—I left a bunch of laundry in the washer for a few days and it got all stanky. I just got the lecture on utility bills, again."

"Okay, later on."

Harper hung up the phone and lay on her bed, gazing up at the ceiling. When she was little, she thought her ceiling looked like the surface of the moon. The granular paint sometimes fell down into her sheets. David called it moondust. She sighed, rolled onto her left side, and dialed Katie's number.

"Hey, guess what?" Katie said. "I got promoted to afternoon desk clerk!"

The Gallaghers must have caller ID. The suddenness of Katie's pronouncement made Harper feel out of step with normal time. "Hello to you, too," Harper said. "But that's great."

"Did something happen?"

"Dwight fired me."

"He figured out you weren't engaged?"

The concern in Katie's voice soothed her. Katie could change in a second. One minute everything was about her; the next minute it was all about you.

Harper nodded into the phone, not trusting her voice.

"Listen, after they gave me the job, two of the other chambermaids quit," Katie said. "Neither of them really spoke English, so they might have actually tried to tell my boss they were leaving, but she didn't understand. Anyway, they'll bump me back to cleaning if we can't find someone else. Do you want me to see if she'll give you the job?"

"Sure," Harper said. "Anything for a paycheck."

•

HARPER WENT FOR an interview at the Motel 6 the following afternoon. Katie must have told the manager that Harper was pregnant because she didn't seem surprised when Harper introduced herself. Mrs. Wood wore a navy blue suit, a striped polyester blouse, and reminded Harper of an old-fashioned school marm. She ushered Harper into a small office behind the check-in desk.

"Katie tells me that you're looking for a job, but I have to tell you that we don't usually hire women who are so far along in a pregnancy."

"I know I look really big, but I'm not due for another two months, until mid-May."

Mrs. Wood looked doubtful. Harper noted the gold rings on her right hand, her French manicure. She wasn't going to pitch in herself.

"I live in the apartments right over there," Harper said. "I'm really happy to work on weekends, and you'd never have a problem with me showing up. My mom works, but I like things to be nice, so I clean our apartment. I'd do a good job." Harper twisted the inside edge of her left sleeve.

"Well, we can try it," Mrs. Wood sighed. "But when you decide to stop working, please let me know as soon as possible. What are you planning to do after the baby's born?"

"I don't know. I'd have to find someone to watch her."

"Well, it would be a relief to have someone who speaks English." Mrs. Wood turned a pencil in her fingers. "Katie really vouched for you. She said you were trying to do the right thing."

Harper nodded, unsure of what to say.

"Let me show you a few things, and if you decide you want to do this, Katie can give you more specific instructions."

As Mrs. Wood showed her the laundry and where the cleaning supplies were kept, Harper wondered what Katie had said about her. Was she trying to do the right thing? Right hadn't really entered into it. She was trying to do whatever wouldn't make her feel worse, or what wouldn't make her feel worse in the future. It wasn't the best way to make a decision, but it was all she could do right now.

•

HARPER HAD TOLD Mrs. Wood the work wouldn't bother her, but her stomach, her general clumsiness, did get in the way. Sometimes, she'd drop something, pick it up, then drop it again. She'd read in a magazine that this had something to do with being pregnant—muscles or ligaments or something got looser. It was a relief to know that it wasn't just her, but it was annoying that she couldn't keep anything in her hands.

It was hard to get down low, to clean the tubs and bases of the toilets. Cleaning up after her mother wasn't fun, but cleaning up after strangers was worse. They left gooey muffin wrappers on the floor, draped wet towels into unflushed toilets, squashed cigarette butts into soap dishes, dropped snotty tissues on the floor. She wore gloves while she cleaned. Her life had been boiled down to necessities: eating, getting money, getting sleep.

Working as a maid was different than working at Dunkin' Donuts, where the customers had actually talked to her. At the motel, people acted as if she were invisible. One morning, as Harper pushed her cart down the hall, a woman in a tweed jacket and beige pants, talking on her cell phone, bumped into her. She didn't say "excuse me," or even acknowledge that she'd bumped into Harper. She just carried on her conversation. "Yes, it's spelled like Milan, but they call it MYlan, can you imagine?" The woman laughed as if it were the most ridiculous thing she'd ever heard. Harper felt a flash of anger. She hated this place herself, but what did the woman think—that the people who worked here had been airlifted from someplace else?

•

BY EASTER, HARPER had become some other version of herself. As she had grown larger, it seemed that there was more of her, literally, that had to deal with the outside world. Part of her still wanted to drop out of school, disappear, but the school principal and counselors continued to be matter-of-fact and didn't present dropping out as a possibility. If she wanted to stop coming to school, which they didn't recommend, she had to draw up an Educational Goals Plan and give deadlines for when she'd complete these goals. Her mother would have to sign off on the plan, monitor Harper's deadlines, and attend school meetings. Harper had never imagined that it would be easier to attend school hugely pregnant than it would be to drop out. In meetings with the school counselor, a surprisingly upbeat young woman, Harper filled out a questionaire and felt humiliated that her answer to almost every question was "I don't know." Her private imaginings—working in a little store where she could have her baby with her, moving through the sunny air with a child on her back—seemed ridiculous when faced with warnings about her future.

How was she planning to support her child? Her mother asked almost every day, implying that any idea of Harper's would be ridiculous. At school, the counselor asked with a sense of possibility, but the possibilities didn't have anything to do with the kind of life she wanted for herself. Did she want to learn medical transcription? Data entry? How to cut hair? Would she like to work as a secretary? Harper wondered if she looked like the type of person who wanted to do those things. She tried to think about what she'd envisioned before she got pregnant. She would sound simple-minded if she said that she wanted to live somewhere pretty, have friends to talk to. Harper could imagine a place in the country where it didn't cost a lot to live—but she didn't know what kind of job she could do.

The principal encouraged her to see how much schoolwork she could do before the baby came. Maybe she could work ahead and finish her schoolwork by the end of the year.

·

AS THE WEATHER turned, became warmer, Harper missed moving freely among other people. She had thought of herself as small and desirable, but now, she was weighted. When she walked down the road, nobody honked or hollered or whistled; she was just a girl lumbering up the road.

One morning, as Harper arrived at the motel, Mrs. Wood beckoned her into the office. A sense of dread rolled over her.

"Harper, how long do you plan to keep working?"

"Right up to the time, if I can," Harper said. She waited for a moment, wondering if Mrs. Wood wanted anything else.

"Are you sure you're all right?"

"Yeah, actually I am. It's good for me to get out." Harper knew it was a ridiculous thing to say, as if cleaning hotel rooms was actually getting out, but she skipped school on days she couldn't bear to go, and sitting in her dark apartment depressed her.

"Well, you've been dependable, so we're glad to have you."

Harper felt lighter, knowing Mrs. Wood was pleased. That day, someone who'd stayed for two nights even left her a tip.

·

AT THE END of her shift, she cut through the mobile home park instead of walking around it. She'd taken to doing this over the past few weeks, saying hello to whoever she passed. The old woman with a blue trailer, on the side near the motel, was preparing a garden. She had a large black compost bin and was trying to stir inside it with a pitchfork, but she wasn't tall enough or strong enough to manage. She looked like a clumsy witch. She always announced she was waiting for someone: a man to deliver railroad ties so she could make a raised garden bed, a friend to deliver grass clippings to her bin. She waved her cane in greeting whenever Harper walked by.

•

NOW, WHEN HARPER woke in the morning, she had to sit up slowly. She used her left arm to push herself up, rested on the edge of her bed, and felt a pressing inside her, sharp above her pubic bone. Dr. Watkins said it was because the baby's head was down, just as it should be, and that the time was getting close.

She wondered about Nate, although he had faded in her memory. What would he do, if he knew? It was hard to think of him as an adult, although he did seem responsible—for someone without responsibilities. Now that she wasn't at Dunkin' Donuts, he wouldn't know how to find her, even if he wanted to.

The baby kicked and moved, especially after she ate milk and cookies, and although the kicking didn't feel good, the movement made her feel peculiarly alive. She liked knowing the baby was a girl. Even though Dr. Watkins said the sonogram wasn't for sure, she thought it was right. Harper wished she could feel truly happy, but the possibility that the baby would be too much, that she would have to give her up, kept her from feeling content. She'd said she wanted to keep it, but maybe she couldn't do it. Maybe everyone was right.

•

HARPER WENT TO school just enough to stay out of trouble; sitting through classes seemed pointless. One Friday, when she'd stayed home, Janet and Katie called at lunchtime and said they were coming to get her as soon as they got out of class. It was a warm afternoon, the weather bright, the trees green. When they pulled out of the apartment parking lot, Janet bouncing in her seat to a song on the radio, Harper re-membered a year ago, when everything seemed open and limitless in front of her. They drove through the spring light, the yellow-green leaves overhead, and ended up at the old Edison place, where they sat on a stone wall near the ravine.

"We've got to go to garage sales and get baby stuff for you," Katie said.

Harper pulled a sapling branch toward her and ran her hand over it, stripping the leaves from it. "I don't want a bunch of stuff some other kid has thrown up on."

"Well, don't buy an old high chair then. You wouldn't need one at first, anyway. Is your mother going to buy you a crib?"

"She's not buying anything. She's still hoping I'll give the baby away."

"Do you want to?" Janet asked.

Katie looked at Harper, waiting.

Harper gazed down into the overgrown ravine below. "Only when I'm scared."

They didn't ask how often this was.

"Where's it going to sleep?" Katie asked.

"The old fashioned way. On some blankets in a drawer."

"Maybe we can find a bassinet," Katie said.

"You need a car seat," Janet said.

"I don't have a car."

"But if your mother wants you to come to the store with her, you're not going to get a babysitter, so you need a car seat," Janet said.

"I guess you're right," Harper said. They were oblivious about some things, but so often they pointed out things she wouldn't have realized herself.

"There's a three-family garage sale near my house tomorrow," Katie offered.

"Is it near Matt's?"

"Not too close."

"I don't want to see him or his Mom."

"They're not really garage sale types, are they?"

The following morning, Janet picked Harper up while her mother was still asleep. Another bright day, a day to be outside, and Harper was pleased to have somewhere to go.

"New barrette?" Harper grinned as she got into the car.

"This?" Janet touched a powder blue barrette dotted with rhinestones. "My sister found it in a vintage shop in Toledo. Or maybe it wasn't a vintage shop, it was just Toledo."

Harper laughed. "All you need is some cat-eyed glasses."

"Leopard skin tights!" Janet grinned and put her foot on the gas.

They turned toward Milan, passing over the freeway, a stretch of fields broken up by warehouses, a gas station that had gone out of business. They passed the construction site where the strip mall was supposed to be, but the site, weedy and barren, was still criss-crossed by tire tracks hardened in the mud.

When they pulled into Katie's driveway, the weather seemed brighter. Azaleas lined the pathway, a profusion of magenta. Katie's youngest brother was in the garage, studying an overturned lawn mower. He stared at Harper, then went back to puttering with his tools.

"I hate this," Harper said.

"What?"

"Dealing with parents. Wondering what they'll say."

Janet rang the doorbell, and they heard Katie's feet pounding down the stairs. She opened the door and ushered them in. "Come in a minute. I've got to get my purse," Katie said.

Katie's house was large and spacious, but stepping into the front hall, Harper felt closed in. Katie led them through the living room, where Mr. Gallagher, wearing sweatpants and reading glasses, sat in a recliner reading *Money* magazine. He looked up when the girls came in.

"Morning girls," he said. He glanced at Harper over his

reading glasses before going back to his magazine.

They walked into the kitchen where Katie's mother was washing up.

"Hi there," she called over the sound of running water. Mrs. Gallagher wore a zippered sweatshirt and matching yellow pants, clean white sneakers. "Well, Harper, look at you." She rinsed the soap off her hands, reached for a towel, and came around the kitchen island. Harper flinched. "Oh sweet, well, your timing might be better, but it's done now, eh?"

Harper smiled tightly, unsure of what to say.

"Katie says you're planning to keep the baby."

"Yes, it seems like it."

"Well, make no mistake. If Katie got herself pregnant I'd tan her hide—"

"Mom!"

"What do you expect me to say? Harper, wouldn't it be silly if we pretended you weren't pregnant? Look at you, you're about to pop! Listen, I know you're going around to sales for practical things, but I got you a little something."

Harper looked at Katie, who gave her an I-don't-believe-my-mother look. Mrs. Gallagher left the room then returned with a wrapped package. "Here," she said. "Open it."

"Mrs. Gallagher, you didn't have to."

"If you're going to have a baby, you might as well enjoy it. Katie said your mother hasn't been exactly perky."

The wrapping paper, shiny white with an opalescent sheen, was expensive, different than any she'd seen before. Harper gently tore it open to find three Carter's outfits. The first was a pair of pajamas with pale green and yellow houses, lines of pink smoke coming out of the chimneys, as if drawn in crayon. The other packages were something called "onesies" with pastel decorations.

Harper touched the tiny snaps. The clothes were so new

and clean and sweet she thought she'd weep.

"These onesies are really handy," Mrs. Gallagher said. "In summer, they're all a baby needs, and they also help keep the diapers on. Do you know if you're using cloth or disposable?"

"I'm not sure." Harper swallowed the tears in her throat. She didn't want to admit she hadn't thought about it. She didn't know they still had cloth diapers.

"Do you have a washing machine in your apartment?"

"There's one downstairs, in the basement."

"You'll probably want disposable then. They're more expensive, but it's hard to carry diaper buckets up and down the stairs. You don't want to have to fool with that." Mrs. Gallagher smiled at Harper and turned to set plates in the sink.

Harper felt as if she had been assumed into a new role, with a vocabulary all its own: onesies, cloth diapers, diaper buckets. "Mrs. Gallagher, thanks a lot. This was really nice for you to do." Her eyes stung; she didn't want to cry.

Mrs. Gallagher turned and put her hands on Harper's shoulders. Harper couldn't look at her. "Harper, look. I don't mean to make light of this, but face it, darling, this is the oldest story in the world."

Harper nodded, swallowing the knot in her throat. She wanted to lean into Mrs. Gallagher and cry, but she stood still, wiping her eyes. She didn't know what else to say. She gathered up her package. Then she and Janet and Katie went back outside, into the bright, revealing light.

12

HARPER WOKE ON a Tuesday morning in May feeling crampy, a bit uncomfortable, but it didn't feel like what anyone would call contractions. She wanted to shower before going to the motel, but decided, since she'd just be cleaning anyway, to shower when she came home. It felt good to get clean then, washing away the feeling of cleaning other people's dirt, but these days, even standing in warm water made her tired. Getting in and out of the shower, bending over, drying her hair–everything took effort now. She couldn't wait until she could move freely again. She sat down on her bed and wondered if she should stay home. Maybe the other chambermaids could get it all done. Harper calculated in her head: five hours at \$5.36 per hour. Almost thirty dollars. She didn't want to lose the income.

She lumbered over to the motel, cutting through the trailer park. The frog lady waved her cane, and Harper waved back. She felt lucky to have work so close by, especially since she couldn't hurry, even if she wanted to.

She was cleaning a bathroom, leaning over the toilet, when

she felt something warm and wet between her legs. She stood up. Was it her water breaking? Her pants stuck to her inner thighs; it felt disgusting. She stepped into the tub because she didn't want to mess up the floor she'd just cleaned.

Grabbing a towel from the rack, she put it between her legs, then hobbled to the phone and called the front desk. At her last checkup, Dr. Watkins asked if she had a birth plan. Harper said that Katie and Janet both had cell phones. That was her birth plan.

"Will you get Mrs. Wood, please?" The line clicked as Harper was transferred. Muzak filled her ears. What if she was stuck on hold with Muzak when she was going to have a baby? For a terrible moment she thought it could happen—no one would know she was in labor.

Suddenly, walking to the front desk seemed a huge distance. The phone clicked again, and Harper caught her breath. "Mrs. Wood, my water just broke. You have Katie's cell number, don't you? Could you call Katie and have her come and get me?"

"Oh! Harper, of course. I'll call her and be right down."

Harper took a bunch of towels and put them under her, then sat in the arm chair. The contractions were starting, she could feel them. She had wondered if labor would be boring, if she would want to watch TV between contractions; the idea seemed ridiculous now. She wanted quiet.

She tried to take a deep breath. Nothing hurt yet, but her body felt different, as if she couldn't control it. Sitting in the chair, holding onto the arms, the contractions felt like waves coming at her. Once, a long time ago, her mother had taken her and David to the beach in New Jersey where they stayed with her cousins. Harper must have been nine or ten; she couldn't really swim, but she played in the waves while her mother sat with her aunt, talking and smoking on the beach. When Harper paddled into the deeper water, the waves knocked her over, tumbling her in the current. Swallowing a mouthful of briny water, she sputtered and choked, tried to catch her breath. The water wasn't deep, but she couldn't touch bottom, and it was hard to get back to the shore; the tide kept pulling her back out. She knew how to dog paddle, how to keep her head above water, but it was hard to watch for waves and stay afloat. Every time she got close to shore, another wave tumbled her over, somersaulting her in the green, salty dark. David, in the distance, didn't know she was scared. He ducked under the waves, and she tried to do what he did, but she wasn't as tall, couldn't get her footing, and her arms and legs grew tired. She tried to get below the waves, but it was scary, holding her breath, hoping they didn't tumble her. She felt like that now, the contractions, which didn't really hurt, were like huge scary waves coming at her.

Mrs. Wood hurried into the room. "Are you all right?"

"I think so. Is Katie coming?"

"She just got out of class. She'll be right here."

"Sorry I didn't finish the room."

Mrs. Wood smiled. "You're a crazy kid." She sat down on the end of the bed and took Harper's hand.

"It doesn't hurt," Harper said, "but I can't really talk. I feel like everything's rushing at me."

"It's okay," Mrs. Wood said. "You'll be just fine."

Katie burst into the room, her cheeks flushed.

"I don't know if I can walk to the car," Harper said.

"You have to." Katie leaned over and put her shoulder under Harper's arm. Mrs. Wood got on the other side. Everything outside Harper's body seemed faraway. She got into the front seat of Katie's car, and as Katie drove, Harper tried to breathe.

"Are you okay?" Katie said.

"It's kind of scary."

"We'll be there soon."

When they got to the hospital, Katie pulled up to the Emergency entrance. "I'll get someone to help you," she said, and ran into the front door. Harper sat, staring at the red brick wall until the bricks started moving with the rhythm of her breath. The expansion and contraction of the bricks scared her, so she focused on an old couple making their slow way to the door. Katie returned a few minutes later with an aide and a wheelchair.

"How far apart are your contractions?" the woman asked.

"I have no idea," Harper gasped. "They seem like they're right on top of each other."

When they got inside, Katie filled in Harper's forms, and Harper reached up to the counter to sign them. The receptionist glanced at the papers, then looked at Harper over her half-glasses.

"Is this your labor partner?" the receptionist asked.

Harper wasn't sure what to say. She nodded, yes.

"Since you're a minor, we have to get your parents here in case of complications."

"There's just my mother."

"We need to give her a call."

"I don't want her here."

"I'm sorry, miss. As a minor, it's necessary."

"I DON'T WANT HER HERE!"

"There's no need to shout, miss. She doesn't have to be in the delivery room, but we do need to contact her."

Harper felt a strange sense of demand. She could ask for, should ask for, anything she wanted. As the receptionist looked over her forms, Harper tugged on Katie's sleeve so Katie would bend down to her. "Pretend to call her, but call a wrong number. I don't want my mother here."

"I can call her," Katie said brightly.

"We're responsible for notifying the guardian," the nurse

said. "Please turn off your cell phone."

"Where's Dr. Watkins?" Harper called.

"He'll be here shortly."

A nurse wheeled her into a room. Later, Harper could barely remember how she got out of her clothes and into a bed where she could half sit up. The nurse took Harper's blood pressure, used a stethoscope to listen to the baby's heart. "Your baby's heartbeat is strong, and everything is just fine. Let's check your dilation." She parted Harper's knees and examined her briefly. "You're doing well, about seven centimeters, coming right along. Dr. Watkins will be here any minute."

Katie looked stunned, her mouth half-open, as if she were watching something moving at terrific speed. Harper couldn't stand for anyone else to be scared right now. When Dr. Watkins arrived, she felt relieved.

"Hello there, my dear. I heard your water broke. Ready to have a baby?"

Harper nodded, then felt a contraction coming on and couldn't speak. After a minute, she said, "I don't want my mother here."

"You don't want her in the room with you—even now?"

"No!" she gasped.

"You want your friend here."

"Yes."

Katie's cheeks were bright red; she'd been uncharacteristically quiet. "Do you want me to call Janet?" she whispered.

"I think we have enough people here," Dr. Watkins said.

Harper couldn't think beyond her own body. She felt as if a shower curtain of clear plastic separated her from everyone around her; other people seemed blurry.

The nurse walked back into the room, and Dr. Watkins took her aside, murmured something to her, then turned to Harper. "When your mother arrives, we'll tell her she can wait outside. We'll simply say it's because we need to concentrate."

Harper nodded and tried to sit up. Nothing felt comfortable. She shifted in the bed, but it was hard to move. She lay on her left side for a few minutes, until Dr. Watkins said, "Let's have you on your back for a minute. I want to check your dilation. Then you can sit up again."

His presence was reassuring: his shining head, his fringe of hair, gold-rimmed glasses; he was familiar. She could barely feel him examining her; the contractions eclipsed everything else.

"There isn't time for an epidural, but everything's progressing just fine."

"Do I have to push?"

"No, not yet. Just try to relax, and breathe. I don't mean gasping for air, just deep comfortable breaths. You'll probably be ready in a half-hour or so."

Harper closed her eyes. She felt as if she were spinning away, as if she could die; there was nothing but this overwhelming feeling of being knocked over.

"Harper, look at me," Dr. Watkins said. "Your body will do this; you don't have to think. Just keep breathing, and knowing it's all fine. It's probably good to keep your eyes open, look at Katie, stay present."

Harper felt as if she'd taken a strange drug and couldn't register anything outside herself. She didn't know that doing nothing could go by so quickly. She gripped Katie's hand and stared into her blue eyes, rimmed red from allergies and fear. When Katie wanted to get something to drink, Harper didn't want to let go of her hand.

"I'll be right back, I promise," Katie said.

When Katie walked out of the room, the nurse asked. "Do you want to use the bathroom?"

"Oh, God," Harper said. "I couldn't even take a step."

"I know it seems like that, but sometimes it helps," the

nurse said, "especially if you need to urinate."

"I can't move!" Harper gasped.

A few minutes later, Dr. Watkins came back and checked her again. "I think you're ready to start pushing," he said.

"It doesn't feel like I have a baby inside me," she wailed.

Katie had returned, and Dr. Watkins told her, "You hold her hand and keep looking into her eyes." He turned to Harper. "You're going to push with the contractions now."

"It's all contractions!"

Katie and the nurse were on either side of the bed. Harper was half sitting up, the nurse and Katie holding her bent knees. She would have been embarrassed if there was any room in her to feel such a thing.

"Okay," Dr. Watkins said, "push."

Harper took a deep breath and pushed, but didn't feel anything. "Don't hold your breath," he said. "Take a deep breath. Push again."

"Nothing's happening!" Harper cried.

"Yes it is. Imagine you're pushing the baby's head through a tight turtle-neck shirt. Okay now, push."

Harper could imagine this, but nothing was moving inside her. She took a deep breath and pushed.

"Okay now, you're doing great; I can see the top of the baby's head. One more big push."

Her efforts felt invisible, like struggles in a bad dream. She pushed as hard as she could.

Nothing was happening. She felt dizzy, the room around her surreal.

"Okay, the baby's head is through your cervix. I want you to relax, don't push for just a moment. Just breathe."

Harper felt a sharp pain between her legs. "Oh! Something's happened! It hurts, it hurts, it hurts!"

"It's all right. We're going to slide the shoulders out now."

"It really hurts, it stings, it hurts a lot!" A terrible burning flared between her legs.

Katie's mouth was a huge O, her cheeks pale. She looked as shocked as Harper had ever seen her.

"I want to push, I need to push."

"Okay, go easy now," he said.

"It hurts, it really hurts!"

"It's all right," the nurse said. "It's the baby's shoulders. That's why it hurts. Nothing's wrong. You're doing great."

Harper felt something in her give way, then saw, below her on the bed, the baby's back, the skin slightly loose in soft folds like a puppy.

She leaned forward to see better.

Dr. Watkins picked the baby up and handed it to her. He was smiling broadly. "It's a little girl."

Harper reached for the baby and held it against her. Her eyes were wide open. Her skin had tiny white flakes on it, and she looked, Harper thought, like a little old man. Her chin was tiny and firm, distinct, as if she were already forming her own impressions of the world. Harper studied her cheeks, her little fingernails, her eyebrows, downy brown, barely there. Two little pimples dotted the side of her nose. Harper touched her wrinkled fingers. So small! The baby seemed to gaze at her, although Harper knew she couldn't really see yet. Harper held her, studying her tiny face, and barely registered them cutting the umbilical cord. The baby opened her pink mouth and a tinny squall came out. A little squeak. Harper laughed. Her lips were perfect! Something about that chin, that little mouth—she was a tiny person, someone Harper could know, utterly familiar, and at the same time, her own distinct presence.

"She's amazing," Harper said. "She's a tiny, perfect little girl."

Katie was weeping as if she'd just seen *Titanic* for the first time. "Oh my God," Katie kept saying. "Oh my God."

Dr. Watkins turned, spoke briefly with the nurse, then turned back to Harper. "We need to take her for a minute and weigh her."

"No, don't take her!" Harper said.

"Just right here," he said. "We won't take her out of the room."

Harper sank down in bed as they weighed the baby, who was crying now, the sound muted and thin.

"Six pounds, seven ounces. Perfectly healthy." The nurse wrapped her in a blanket, put a tiny pink cap on her head, and handed her back to Harper. The baby gazed up at her with blue eyes and blinked. She was so light! She fit perfectly into Harper's arms.

"Do you want us to bring your mother in?" the nurse asked.

Harper looked at Dr. Watkins, whose brown eyebrows were raised in question.

He leaned over and whispered, "If you're going to be staying with her for a while, it's best to include her, try to start on the right foot."

Harper nodded, and a minute or two later her mother came into the room. She stood a few feet from the bed and looked at Harper holding the baby.

"Tiny little thing," her mother said.

"Yes."

"Are you staying for a few days?"

"I think they only keep me overnight."

"Did you call those folks in Cleveland?"

Harper just looked at her.

"Well, you should decide soon," her mother said. "I hope you bought diapers." And she walked out of the room.

Suddenly, Harper felt muffled, exhausted. She ran her fingers over the baby's cheeks, touched her downy eyebrows, kissed her little forehead. Her baby, her own. Dr. Watkins followed her mother out of the room. When he returned, he was frowning.

"What did you say to her?" Harper asked.

"That she should make sure to bring an infant car seat when she comes tomorrow." He turned to Katie, who was blowing her nose, still visibly shaken. "Katie, you've been great, and I'd like it if you could stay around for a little bit. Maybe you could get yourself a snack, then come back and hold the baby while I stitch Harper up."

"Is that what hurt at the end?" Harper asked.

"Yes, you didn't tear too badly, but a little. I'll numb you up before I do it."

"It's a little late for that, don't you think?"

He glanced up, saw Harper was grinning, and he smiled.

The nurse came back and stood at the head of the bed. "We have a nursery on the second floor, if you'd like us to take her, so you can rest."

Harper looked up, afraid, and shook her head.

"We can also bring a bassinet in here, so she can be in the room with you," the nurse said.

"When I'm done being stitched, can I see her from my bed?"

"Yes," the nurse said. "She'll be right here."

"I really need to use the bathroom," Harper said. "Can I do that now?"

"Of course," the nurse said.

Harper pulled a robe around herself and got out of bed carefully. The bathroom was attached to her room, only a few yards away, but it felt strange to stand on the cool linoleum floor. She hobbled to the bathroom, flicked on the light, and a loud fan came on. She looked for another switch, to see if she could have the light on without the rough sound of the fan, but there was only one switch.

She sat down, breathed out, and tried to pee. Nothing happened. Oh, she was so full and uncomfortable, but nothing came out of her. What was wrong with her? She turned off the light, hoped the quiet would help. Nothing. Harper started to weep. She needed to pee so badly, but couldn't. It was a terrible feeling. She turned on the light, the fan buzzing like some kind of torture, and she sat there, tears running down her cheeks. Harper sat on the toilet for almost twenty minutes, her bladder impossibly full, hurting, but somehow her body wouldn't release itself. Finally, the nurse knocked on the door and told her it was all right, this happened a lot. They could give her a catheter if she was really uncomfortable. "Just give me some time, okay?" Harper called through the door.

Finally, she was able to trickle a tiny bit out of herself. She couldn't believe it, a trickling after all that was in her. She tried to breathe, let it all come out of her, but it took ages, sitting there, trying to empty herself.

•

WHILE SHE WAS being stitched, Harper thought how strange it was that Dr. Watkins could be doing such a thing to her, and she didn't even care. On the other side of the room, Katie sat in a rocking chair holding the baby.

When Dr. Watkins had finished, he washed his hands and turned to Harper.

"I have patients this afternoon, so I'm going back to my office. The nurses here will take good care of you. If I don't see you later today, I'll make sure to see you before you check out tomorrow."

"Thanks so much. I just can't believe everything."

He smiled, and Harper could tell that he was happy for her, but sensed he knew more than he was saying. He looked at Katie, holding the sleeping baby. "You can believe it. She's lovely and healthy. You did a wonderful job, Harper."

After he left, Katie carried the baby over and set her in the bassinet. She sat down next to Harper on the bed.

"Thanks, Katie."

"I have to say, there were some gross parts, but that was the most amazing thing I've ever seen."

"Don't tell anyone about the gross parts, okay?"

"I won't."

"I can't believe I was all naked and bloody and I didn't even care."

"You were really brave."

"I didn't feel brave."

"I had no idea it was like that."

"I didn't either." Both of them started laughing, and then, as she took a deep breath, Harper started to weep. Katie bent down to hug her, and Harper felt Katie's hot tears on her neck.

After Katie left, Harper felt exhausted, her whole body heavy, as if she were wearing one of those lead aprons they made you wear at the dentist. The baby dozed. She was so still it was hard to tell if she was breathing. Harper sat up, afraid that something was wrong. She felt too tired to stand up, and couldn't quite reach to put her hand on the baby's chest. She rang for the nurse.

"Is she okay? Can you check her?"

The nurse walked over, pulled the blanket down a little so Harper could see the baby's chest moving. She felt for the baby's pulse on her tiny wrist.

"This is what babies do after birth. They nap for a few hours. It's hard work being born. You should rest now, too."

•

HARPER WISHED SHE could stay in the hospital for weeks. She closed her eyes, dozed, but couldn't really sleep. Everything felt surreal, as if she were hovering above her body.

As she shifted, tried to get comfortable, she replayed the birth in her mind, saw again her first glimpse of the baby's naked back, the folds of her skin.

Late in the afternoon, a nurse came in and told her that, when the baby woke up, a lactation specialist would come in and tell Harper about breast-feeding.

"I don't think I can take in any information. This has been the longest day ever."

"Don't worry. What she tells you will be useful, not hard to remember."

Just as Harper was falling asleep, the baby started to cry. Bleary, Harper sat up. She wasn't sure what to do. A different nurse came in, moving briskly. "Let's see how she does with nursing." She helped Harper sit up, put pillows behind her, a thick pillow under her left arm. The nurse reached into the bassinet, then handed the baby to Harper.

Harper lifted the baby toward her breast. Her nipple was too wide to fit into the baby's mouth.

"Here," the nurse said. She put her cool hand under Harper's breast. "You want to get your whole nipple in her mouth. You'll be less sore that way. If she only gets part of it, she can't latch on properly. When she opens her mouth to yawn or cry, just put your breast in her mouth."

The baby was angry now, and when she opened her mouth to wail, Harper held her close, put her hand under her breast, and stuffed her nipple into the baby's mouth. The baby closed her mouth, began to suck, and the texture of Harper's nipple changed: the smooth aureole tightened, the skin rumpled and contracted. The baby had the whole nipple in her mouth. Harper could hardly believe it.

"There she goes," the nurse said. "Your milk probably won't come in until tomorrow, and you'll know when it does—your breasts will be really full. But for now, the baby is getting colostrum. It's got all kind of nutrients, and it's really good for her immune system. Even if it doesn't seem like she's getting a lot, she's getting something very important."

Harper watched the baby's cheek, her rhythmic sucking, her eyelids so delicate that her heartbeat seemed to pulse in them. "It's amazing that she knows what to do."

"Sucking is comforting for babies. It's why people use pacifiers, or kids suck their thumbs. Some babies even suck their thumbs in utero." The nurse looked down at Harper. "You're doing great here. I've got to go down the hall and check on someone, but I'll be back in a few minutes, okay?"

Harper touched the wisps of dark hair on top of the baby's head. She'd never felt anything so soft. This must be why babies had smushy little noses, so they could nurse and breathe at the same time. The baby sucked and snuffled, animal-like, absorbed.

When the nurse came back in, she said, "Why don't you switch sides now?"

"I don't think she wants to let go," Harper said. The baby sucked rapidly, her tiny mouth busy and intent. "How do I get her off?"

"Don't just pull—it'll hurt. Sometimes you have to put a finger in her mouth, kind of break the seal."

Harper put a finger in the side of the baby's mouth. Her little jaws were working steadily, but Harper managed to break the suction and pop her off. The baby looked startled for a moment, then started to cry.

"Okay, switch sides now."

With the baby wailing, it was hard to get arranged: turning her to the other side, holding her neck, arranging a pillow for support. She'd been happy, and then she was interrupted. The baby's crying was like a finger on a doorbell or a phone ringing: Harper felt she had to do something.

As the baby opened her mouth to wail, Harper stuffed her

right nipple into it. She started sucking. Harper giggled. "She's pretty funny," Harper said.

"You're both doing a great job. She's a good nurser. Some babies have trouble—they're too sleepy after the birth—or some women are too hesitant. They overthink it."

Harper felt a tinge of pride. She was good at something that other women weren't. Her baby was naturally good at this.

"Now, I'll give you one simple guideline."

Harper looked up. "I don't think I can remember anything else today."

"This isn't hard, but it's important, and not everyone would say it. I'm off tonight, and I might not see you tomorrow."

"Okay."

"Some people, especially older women who bottle-fed their babies, will tell you that you need to get your baby on a schedule. But you don't put a breastfed baby on a schedule. Babies just want to be held and nursed, so you can nurse her as much as you're comfortable with. It cuts into your sleep, cuts into everything really, but if you nurse her whenever she seems hungry, it will soothe her, make her feel cared for and wanted. Sometimes she might not nurse for long, but if you give babies what they need, I think they're happier. In the beginning it will feel like nursing her is all you're doing, but in the long run, holding her a lot, nursing her, will make her feel more secure."

•

AT NIGHT, THE hospital was quiet. The baby slept next to her bed. Harper could call a nurse if she needed something, but all she wanted was water, and they had left a pitcher by her bed. Harper wished for something sweet and cold and tart: orange sherbet. Tomorrow, when she left, she would get some. The baby squeaked, then gave a little cry. Harper looked up from her pillow and waited to see if the baby really wanted something. The crying continued, and Harper sat up, reached over, and oh, it was hard to make sure she had the back of her delicate stem neck. It was too far to reach. Carefully, Harper got out of bed so she could pick her up more easily. Once she was holding her, it was hard to get back in bed with the baby in her arms, rearrange herself, get a pillow underneath her for a prop, but finally she was able to pull up her nightshirt, bring the baby to her breast. The baby opened her mouth, closed it around Harper's nipple, then quieted. The simple, physical equation seemed like a miracle: the baby cried, Harper put her breast in the baby's mouth, the baby quieted. It had never occurred to Harper that she would have the capacity to make someone happy. She had been unhappy herself, and wanted relief, but she had not considered that she could make another person feel better. She'd made Matt happy when she had sex with him, but that was different, partly because she felt responsible for his desire.

Harper knew that taking care of a baby would get more complicated than this, but the simplicity of this comfort felt good. She had considered her breasts only in terms of how they looked. Now she knew what they were for: warmth, softness, comfort, food. No wonder people were so preoccupied with them.

She had to choose a name before she left the hospital. She hadn't discussed names with anyone. She'd thought of 'August,' for when the baby was conceived, but realized it was foolish. It was May now, and everyone would ask: why would you call her August? Then they would count back nine months, realize, and it would seem stupid. She liked 'Natalie,' the way it sounded, the way it echoed 'Nate,' but when she imagined meeting him in the future, telling him, it felt creepy and grasping, as if she'd been trying, alone, to forge an artificial bond. She had briefly considered something bold and dramatic, like 'Zelda,' but she had learned about F. Scott and Zelda Fitzgerald in English class and didn't want to name the baby after someone crazy.

Harper wanted a name that was sunny and open and happy. "Anna," she said aloud. It seemed like a good name for a little girl.

When people suggested adoption, they said: it's best for the baby if you give it up early, let it bond with its new parents, but that was wrong. What she was doing now was good for Anna. All Anna wanted was to be held and nursed, and Harper could do that. Something occurred to Harper, clear as anything: if she decided it was all too much, she could give Anna up, but if Harper gave her up without really trying, if she signed the papers and made the Anderssons the parents, she couldn't get her back, and that would be terrible. A yawing grief would follow her wherever she went. Harper wanted Anna, this closeness, this warmth; she was going to keep her. She didn't care what anybody said.

•

THE FOLLOWING MORNING, as soon as visiting hours started, Janet hurried into the room. "Oh, look at her! I can't believe you called Katie instead of me!"

Late last night, Harper had thought this might be a sore spot. Janet moved toward the bassinet, leaning over the baby.

"I was at the motel, and Mrs. Wood tried Katie first."

"It's okay, I'll do other stuff." Janet peered at Anna sleeping in her little blankets. "She looks like Nate," Janet pronounced.

"You really think so?"

"Yeah, I do."

"Look at this," Harper said. She reached down into Anna's blankets and pulled them back so Janet could see Anna's foot. "See that toenail?" She touched the smallest toe on Anna's right foot.

"It's so tiny!" Janet made an isn't-that-cute face.

"No, look closer. See how the toenail's kind of split?"

Janet bent down. "There's just a tiny line. What'd she do? Stub her toe inside you?"

"Nate's toenail is just like that."

"No way!" Janet stood up.

"Really, it is." Having said it aloud, Harper felt stunned by the concreteness of this. She covered Anna's legs so they wouldn't get cold.

Janet set a large gift bag on Harper's bed. "For you!"

Harper grinned and pulled out a green nylon shoulder bag with a wide bottom.

"It's a diaper bag. You'll need it for carrying stuff. Plus, look at this." Janet pulled a folded mat from the side of the bag. "This is so that, wherever you are, you have a place to change her."

"Janet, thanks so much."

"Look inside!"

Harper reached into the diaper bag and pulled out a tiny tie-dyed T-shirt, pink and pale blue, shot with white lines. "Oh, it's perfect." She ran her fingers over the wavy lines and started to weep. "I'm such a fuck-up, what am I going to do?"

Janet hugged her. "You'll take care of her. You'll spend the summer feeding her and changing diapers, and figure out your next step in the fall. I can't wait until she gets more hair. I'm going to start buying her barrettes."

Harper laughed, imagining Janet plastering Anna with ridiculous barrettes. "Janet, thanks so much. I really am sorry I didn't call you. I know you wanted to be here, but I felt sort of panicky; they said they had to call my mother, and I kind of lost it. I didn't want her in the room, and there wasn't time for any drugs or anything, so it was just hard to think."

"It's okay," Janet said, hugging her. "It's all going to be just fine."

•

HARPER TRIED TO rest while Anna napped. When Anna
woke and cried, Harper picked her up to nurse her, but she
nursed for only a few minutes, her little mouth puckered pink,
before falling asleep at Harper's breast.

When her mother walked into the room, Harper smelled
smoke.

"Okay," her mother said. "They told me to bring some fresh
clothes, and I got them here. Let's go."

Harper looked up, startled. "Dr. Watkins said he wanted to
talk to us first." Her mother pursed her mouth. "I've got to get
back to work."

A nurse was walking down the hall, and Harper called out
to her. "Excuse me, can you tell Dr. Watkins that my mother is
here?"

"Yes, sure." The nurse hurried away.

Harper took the bag of clothes and headed for the bathroom to get dressed. She didn't want to leave her mother alone
with Anna. She left the bathroom door open a tiny bit, so she
could see Anna as she changed. Her mother had taken a seat
near the window. She reminded Harper of a kid at the back of
the classroom, dying to get out to recess.

"It's nice having a baby in this weather. You can get outside.
Your brother was born in January, and I couldn't get out at all.
I was always afraid I'd slip on the ice or something when I was
carrying him." She turned to look at Harper as she stepped out
of the bathroom. "You, born in August! Being nine months
pregnant in summer was torture."

Harper zipped up her baggy jeans, which were looser now,
although not quite as loose as she'd hoped.

Dr. Watkins came into the room, carrying Harper's chart.
"Well, how's everyone here?"

"Good," Harper said.

He leaned over to look at Anna, whose eyelids fluttered,

half-awake. Her lips formed a perfect little bow.

"She's a beautiful baby," he declared. "And Harper, just for the record, her Apgar scores are excellent." He sat down in a chair next to the bed. "Now, do you have any questions before we release you? Things you want to know?"

Harper sat on the bed, so she could see Anna as they talked. "The nurse explained to me about keeping her belly button clean, that the little bit of umbilical cord will drop off. I know we have hydrogen peroxide."

"And they talked to you about putting her to sleep on her back, didn't they?"

"Yes, or on her side when she's bigger."

He turned to Harper's mother. "Did you bring a car seat with you?"

"Sure I did."

He turned back to Harper. "You need to be careful, if you move it between different cars, that you strap it in really well. Of course, you'll see the instructions, but you never, ever, put it in the front seat."

"Because of airbags," Harper said.

"That's right. So, Harper, Mrs. Canaday, before Harper checks out, a few things to keep an eye on. Harper, you may be feeling fine, energetic even, but it's important not to overdo anything physical in the next two weeks. Let your body rest. It's natural that you'll bleed for a few days, perhaps a week or so. You have some sanitary napkins at home, I hope." He glanced at Mrs. Canaday. "But if you have any bleeding that's more than usual, or you feel lightheaded, you must come to see me immediately."

Harper understood that, although he was talking to her, he was making sure her mother heard this as well. His tone offered protection, although she knew this feeling would only extend as far as his presence. "I heard your mother mentioning the seasons. This is a nice time of year to have a baby, and sun is good, Anna won't get jaundiced that way. But you want to be careful that she doesn't get too much sun. If you're outside on a bright day, she should have a hat to protect her eyes and head. When the weather gets warmer, you have to watch for sunburn. Sun lotion isn't good for infants. They get it in their mouths too easily, so the best thing is to keep them covered up. Have little light clothes, or a very light blanket you can put over the baby carrier, just to keep her shielded from the sun." He looked back and forth between them. "Any questions?"

Harper looked down and touched Anna's cheek. "My milk hasn't come in yet, and the nurse said I'll know when it happens, but what if it doesn't? What if she's nursing and not getting anything?"

"It only seems like that in the beginning. Let's see . . ." He closed his eyes, seeming to calculate. "If your milk hasn't come in by tomorrow afternoon, you call us. The most important thing is for you to drink plenty of fluids—not soda pop, but water, water mixed with juice, lemonade, that kind of thing. You need to be properly hydrated in order to make milk. Right now, she's getting nutrients that are important for her immune system, and nursing her will help your milk come in. I'm sure you'll be fine." He turned to Harper's mother. "Questions Mrs. Canaday?"

"So the baby is healthy?"

Dr. Watkins turned to face her. "Yes, she is. And on that note, it's best if you don't smoke around the baby. Second-hand smoke can trigger childhood asthma and a host of other problems."

"Are you telling me that I can't smoke in my own home?"

A minute ago it had all been fine, now it felt as if the walls were caving in. Harper twisted the cuff of her sleeve and wished Dr. Watkins would just be quiet—her mother would only get more obstinate. He looked surprised, as if he wasn't used to being contradicted so bluntly.

"I'm saying it's not a good idea. It would be nice if you could step out on the porch to have a cigarette. It's also important not to smoke in the car. It's a much more concentrated situation. You're really forcing the baby to smoke."

"I'm not stupid—I get the problem with the cancer sticks, but I don't plan to change my life just because my daughter got knocked up." Her mother reached for her purse, as if she'd light up right there.

"You're just being mean because you want me to give Anna up," Harper said.

"Oh, 'Anna' is it now?" Her mother turned to face them. Her lips were pale, almost the color of her face. "Well, I have a right to my own life. I just got done raising you, and now, when I'm supposed to be getting you out of my hair, you bring this on us. Give me a break."

"Mrs. Canaday, why don't you bring your car around?" Her mother took her purse and marched out of the room.

Dr. Watkins looked at Harper. She was embarrassed by what she read in his expression—a combination of pity and anger.

"Harper, it's hard to know what to say to someone like your mother. How old are you, dear?"

"I turn eighteen on August 2."

"Legally speaking, you're her responsibility until then. But I'd start trying to figure out what else you could do."

A hot fear washed over her.

"I don't necessarily mean giving Anna up, but think about what other living arrangements you could make. Let me ask you something: Anna's father, could he help?"

Hearing her own question, stated so directly, frightened her. She looked down at Anna and touched her cheek. "I think he would," Harper said. "It's more a matter of finding him. He lives out of state, and he's a student himself. He doesn't really have much."

"Well, you might try to make some kind of arrangement with him. I hate to be so blunt, but it doesn't appear that your mother is going to be much help."

Harper nodded, felt tears in her throat, but didn't want to cry.

"I have to see other patients right now, but please call me if you have any questions. You can speak to the nurses as well. Almost all of them have children, so they have lots of experience. One of the aides will help you out with your things."

Harper wished he would stay, put her mother in her place. If only he was someone she could call on for advice: a neighbor or a friend's father. She wanted to hug him, kiss his clean-shaven cheek.

"Okay, bye then." She tried to smile, to pretend she was any new mother taking her baby home.

A woman appeared then, with a wheelchair. "Thanks, but I don't need that," Harper said. The aide was an older woman with short gray hair. It felt too strange to have an old woman help her out of the hospital. Harper picked Anna up, and the aide followed, carrying the diaper bag stuffed with yesterday's clothes. They walked down the cool hallways toward the hospital entrance. Her mother was parked in front, sitting in the driver's seat, staring straight ahead.

Harper opened the front door and the aide set her belongings on the front seat. Carefully, Harper handed Anna to her, so she could check to make sure the car seat was fastened tightly.

Harper opened the back door. The car seat lay on its side, still wrapped in plastic. Her head started to pound and, scanning the back seat, Harper spotted the directions on the floor. The aide waited as Harper unfolded the sectioned pages–Spanish, French, Japanese–trying to find the directions in English.

"This might take a minute," Harper said.

"I've done plenty of this," the aide said. She glanced at Harper's mother in the front seat. "Would you like me to do it?"

Harper nodded, and the aide handed Anna back to her.

"Let's see those directions, just to make sure we get it rigged up with these seatbelts." Glancing at the diagram, she turned her attention to the back seat, threading the seat belt through the right places on the plastic base of the seat. Harper watched carefully and tried not to be distracted by her own embarrassment. Her mother sat like an ugly mannequin, as if she bore no relation to them at all. The aide's rump stuck out of the hot car as she fiddled with the webbed straps.

"There you go!" She tugged on the top, tried to push it from side to side. It seemed secure.

Holding Anna's head and neck, Harper set her in the car seat. It was the smallest kind, for infants, but she still seemed too small for it. Harper fumbled with the wide straps, trying to adjust them, and finally clipped her in. Anna leaned to one side, and Harper grimaced. She needed a towel or little blanket to prop her up. Her mother tapped her fingers on the steering wheel, impatient, and blew out of her mouth. Harper unclipped Anna, reached into her bag and took out the shirt she'd worn yesterday. It wasn't much material, but she rolled it up and placed it by Anna's side to help hold her up. That was better. She clipped her in again. As Harper thanked the aide, the woman touched her shoulder, and Harper felt herself blush. How humiliating, was this how it was going to be—her mother doing the absolute minimum? Harper climbed into the front seat.

As they pulled out of the parking lot, Harper glanced back at Anna, who seemed too delicate to be moving through the world in a steel contraption. Harper wished her mother would drive slowly, not tailgate the car in front of her, but she looked over at her mother—not smoking—she always lit a cigarette as soon as she started the car, and Harper thought it would be better not to say anything right now.

•

AS THEY DROVE in silence, Harper wondered if her mother was really going back to work. Harper had bought diapers a few days ago, but she was hungry and thirsty, and wondered if there was anything to eat at home. As they got close to the grocery store, Harper felt anxious; she had to speak up now. Her mother wouldn't want to run an errand once they got home.

"You know what I really want?"

"What's that?"

"Orange sherbet."

"You're kidding."

"I'm not. I've been craving it since I was at the hospital. Can we stop and get some, and some extra diapers?"

Her mother blew out of her mouth. "Okay," she said, and swerved into the left lane. A car horn blared behind them. A woman in an SUV waved her arms behind the windshield.

Harper's heart thudded. She looked at Anna, who was oblivious. They waited in the left turn lane, traffic speeding toward them, and Harper braced her feet against the floor. Finally, they turned into the parking lot. The SUV gunned past, the driver's lipsticked mouth moving in a silent shout.

"I'll just wait here," Harper said.

Her mother got out, lit a cigarette, then headed across the parking lot. Harper turned around to look at Anna, tilted to one side of the car seat, too little to keep herself upright. Harper smiled, it was almost funny. Her wisps of dark hair were the color of Nate's. The nurse had explained that Anna couldn't see very well yet; everything was blurry shapes and colors. Harper thought how strange it was to be born—one minute you were inside someone, where it was soft and warm and dark, a world of muffled voices, and you didn't know anything at all, you didn't even know the whole world was out here, and then the press of being born when you weren't expecting it. How weird it must be: being squeezed on everywhere, pushed out of warmth, and the next minute everything was loud and bright and clattering—you were picked up, moved around, washed and held, alive in the bright air. She wondered if dying was like that—you thought you were being squeezed out, into nothing, but instead you got born into something large and bright, a world you hadn't even imagined.

13

AS SHE CARRIED Anna into the apartment, Harper saw it through a stranger's eyes. Junk mail littered the table. Her mother's jacket spilled off a chair. Ashtrays heaped with crushed butts and glasses flecked with dried liquid rested in odd groupings. The tinny smell of old beer seeped from cans dotting the room. Her mother must have had a half-assed party last night.

Harper carried Anna into her bedroom, laid her carefully on the bed, then knelt down and pulled a drawer out of her dresser. She'd emptied it a few days ago, thinking it was a perfect size for a baby. She folded three baby blankets, cotton ones, and placed her palm flat to check the cushioning. It would be soft, but not too fluffy. Overly soft beds were dangerous; Anna could suffocate if she turned over, so really, a drawer with a few blankets would be just fine.

Harper set the drawer by her bed. It didn't look very nice, but Anna would be close. She set her in her little bed, just to see how it was, but Anna started to cry. Harper chewed the inside of her cheek. Maybe she didn't like it, or maybe she wanted to be nursed.

Harper carried her into the living room and settled herself on the couch, sitting next to the end so she'd have something to brace her arm against. She pulled up her shirt, pulled down her bra. Anna opened her mouth, found Harper's breast, and started to nurse.

In the kitchen, Harper's mother scooped sherbet into bowls. She set a bowl on the coffee table in front of Harper, but Harper couldn't reach it, or eat it, with Anna nursing. She wanted to ask her mother to set it in the refrigerator or the freezer, but her mother plopped down in the recliner, picked up the remote, and turned on a soap opera. By the time Anna was done, the sherbet had half melted, but Harper didn't care. She lay Anna on a baby blanket on the carpet and shoveled the cold brightness into her mouth. Oh, it was so good! She could eat a gallon of it. Anna blinked and gazed around from her blanket on the floor. Janet had said that you couldn't have too many of these blankets, and Harper hadn't really believed her, but on the day they went to the garage sale Harper had bought a bunch of them. Already she could see that Janet was right.

"I've got to get back to work," her mother said, shifting forward out of her chair.

"Okay."

Her mother paused, waiting for something.

"Thanks for bringing me home."

"It was probably a mistake," her mother said.

"What?"

"Bringing the baby home. You'll just get more attached to her, and it will be harder to give her up."

"I don't want to give her up."

"You'll get sick of it—the diapers, the crying, you can't go out with your friends. And what boys will be interested in you? Can I bring my baby? That's a great date. You'll see."

Plexiglass, Plexiglass, Plexiglass, Harper thought. Her

mother's beak-like lips kept moving, but Harper blotted out her words. What if keeping Anna was a mistake? It was all a mistake.

When her mother left, Harper clicked off the television. Anna dozed in a sunny place on the floor. Harper wanted a shower. Was it safe to leave her here? The sun wasn't in her eyes.

She couldn't roll over. They had no pets, so there was nothing to hurt her. What else? If the phone rang, it might startle her. Harper turned off the ringer and locked the door so no one could come in. She wanted to clean the hospital and its antiseptic smells off her.

Her own bathroom felt comforting. It had been terrible yesterday, sitting on the toilet forever, the loud fan whirring over her. Now, the drum of water on porcelain was soothing; after getting the temperature right, she turned her face towards the warm water. She had just lathered her hair when she heard the sound of babies crying—the cries rushed in on her—a chorus, a multitude washing over her. They came from nowhere, the keening like a terrible force, as if every baby, everywhere in the world, was wailing in the distance, pain and fear blending with the rush of hot water. She stopped and stuck her head outside the shower curtain—she'd left the bathroom door open on purpose. She didn't hear Anna's thin wail in the living room. Turning off the water, just to make sure, Harper shivered as the soap and water dripped down her body. Nothing. Silence. She didn't want to get out with soap in her hair; it would be a mess. She turned on the water again, tipping back her head to rinse out her hair, and heard the ghost cries again, the sound of children wailing. Harper trembled at the chorus of all the newborns in the world, *I'm scared, I'm scared, I'm scared. I hurt, I hurt, I hurt.* Something in her broke open, and Harper started to weep. She held onto the soap dish to keep her balance as she sobbed in the shower. What in the world had she done?

The world was hard and awful and she had brought Anna into it, and Anna had only her, who knew nothing, to stand between her and everything else.

She turned off the water and the sound stopped. She tried to take a deep breath, but her lungs felt tight, as if she couldn't get enough air. Drying off, she ran the towel over her rumpled stomach. She'd thought it would deflate automatically, like a punctured balloon, but it looked more like a slowly withering one. She guessed that getting back to normal would take some time.

She felt wobbly after crying, and moved around the apartment, straightening up while Anna napped. She opened the windows, washed the dishes, wiped things down. In the kitchen, tomato sauce crusted in a pan, and dried noodles stuck to a colander. She set them to soak as she heard Anna waking. Harper nursed her and changed her, putting peroxide on the scab-like stump of umbilical cord, which looked dark and strange against the smooth perfection of her skin.

Anna cried again, and Harper wasn't sure what to do. Her milk still hadn't come in, and she thought it was best if she did what she could, but it was clear that Anna wanted more, more, more. Harper sat down to nurse her again.

By evening, Harper wondered if her mother would come home and make dinner. She checked the refrigerator: beer, a half cup of orange juice, a bottle of wine. She looked in the cupboard. A box of mac and cheese, but no milk. Spaghetti noodles, but there was no sauce left. No bread. In the freezer: ice, sherbet, two packages of frozen green beans. A package of peas.

She hated peas. Harper drummed her fingers on the countertop. Anna was too little to carry to the grocery store, a good mile's walk from here. Harper couldn't go by herself now because how could she manage groceries in a knapsack and hold the baby as well? Her mother was making her point—you can't do this by yourself—and every time Harper asked for something, her mother would rub it in that Harper was a burden, that she had made a stupid mistake. She drank the rest of the orange juice, made some spaghetti and ate it with margarine. She was still hungry.

At eight-thirty, her mother came home with a pizza. Not a frozen one—a take-out one.

The smell was wonderful. Harper had never been so hungry in her life. As soon as she started to eat, Anna cried to be nursed. Harper took two huge bites, burning the top of her mouth, and picked Anna up.

Her mother watched her. "I don't think you have enough milk for that baby. You're feeding her all the time, and it's not enough."

"It takes a while for the milk to come in."

"What if it doesn't?"

"I think she's okay," Harper said. She ran her finger along Anna's arm, which was thin, the skin mottled and red.

"What do you know?" Her mother asked.

In bed that night, Harper couldn't sleep. What if her milk didn't come in? What if Anna was crying because she was dehydrated? By midnight, Harper was exhausted, but Anna was awake, more alert than she'd been all day. When she finally slept, it was for less than an hour, and she woke at odd intervals through the night. After the third time Anna woke up, Harper stopped keeping track. She'd been told that she could lie down to nurse her, but it didn't work. Anna couldn't find her breast; it was hard to get the right position. Finally, Harper picked her up and went into the living room. A yellow metallic light shone from a streetlight outside. She sat in the recliner and tried to nurse Anna again. Harper's nipples were sore, and each time Anna latched on, Harper winced. She dozed in the recliner, holding Anna, and they finally went back to her bedroom as the sky was getting light.

•

WHEN SHE WOKE in the morning, with Anna in the little drawer next to her bed, Harper's chest felt warm and aching. She touched her breasts, swollen and thick. Anna was asleep, her arms flung back, above her head. Harper scurried into the bathroom, lifted her T-shirt, and stared at her breasts; they jutted out as if they belonged to someone else, so full they hurt, and she went back to her bedroom where Anna was just beginning to stir.

Harper sat up on her bed, arranged the pillows behind her, then lifted Anna towards her. With her breasts so swollen and heavy, she didn't know how Anna could get a nipple into her mouth; it would be like trying to suck on a balloon. Harper put her hand under her breast, lifted Anna toward it, and Anna opened her mouth, bird-like, and closed it around her nipple. She hadn't opened her mouth wide enough, and Harper grimaced, wanted to yell, but didn't want to startle her. She stuck her finger in the side of Anna's mouth and popped her off so she could try again. As Anna opened her mouth to wail, Harper brought her close and stuffed her nipple into Anna's mouth. Anna gulped. Harper felt an odd sensation, a tingling on the outside of her breast, like pins and needles, and then she was doing it! Milk bubbled up around Anna's lips. It worked! Anna looked almost surprised. For a moment, she stopped sucking and milk dribbled out of her mouth. Harper wanted to weep with gratitude. Milk, she had milk. Her mother was wrong. She was just fine. She nursed Anna on one breast, then on the other. Her breasts softened, but even after nursing, thin milk leaked from them, and she had to find a washcloth to wipe herself up. She wanted to call the nurse who'd helped her, to tell her it worked, but that would be silly. Privately, she rejoiced. She could do this! Harper lifted Anna to her shoulder and heard a tiny burp.

•

HARPER DIDN'T COME out of her room until after her mother had left. The pizza box was open on the counter; her mother had taken the last two slices for her lunch. Her stomach lurched, as if an elevator had dropped a floor. She was starving. What was she going to do? Janet and Katie couldn't shop for her—Janet had to work after school, and Katie couldn't always use her mother's car. Beyond that, Harper knew it wasn't the kind of thing she could ask—it would seem like an ongoing chore, rather than a favor. They'd done so much already, and she'd have to pay them back when she was trying to save up to get away.

The phone rang, and it was Mrs. Wood, asking if she could stop by to see the baby. "Sure, that would be great," Harper said. She paused and looked around the apartment.

"Mrs Wood? I hate to ask you this, but—"

"What is it, dear?"

"Well, my mother went to work this morning, but there's no food in the apartment. I mean, there's some sherbet, but there's just not . . . I can pay you back. I could give you a check. I know you're my boss, so it's weird to ask if you could pick up some groceries, but I don't know what else to do."

"Harper, of course."

Harper heard the pity in her voice. She was both embarrassed and confirmed when people recognized her mother's meanness. She'd felt the same way when she talked to Dr. Watkins. When she revealed her mother's unkindness, people felt sorry for her, would do things for her, but it felt ugly, cheap, to play on this. Right now, she didn't know what else to do.

"I'll run by the store on my way," Mrs. Wood said.

"I really appreciate it."

Harper scooped a bowl of sherbet for breakfast, the orange brightness so cold and sweet.

•

AFTER CHANGING ANNA, Harper tried to straighten up the apartment. She started to vacuum, but the noise scared Anna. Or maybe it didn't scare her, she was simply hungry again. When Anna cried, Harper nursed her; she didn't know what else to do. A breast in Anna's mouth comforted her immediately. Harper stared at the whorl of her ear, her skin orange in the sunlight. Suck, suck, suck, was all she wanted; she'd nursed just an hour ago. This was what the nurse had meant. All those things that people said were real now. The nurse had said, "It will seem like this is all you're doing," and Harper had thought she was exaggerating. Clearly, she wasn't.

Anna's soft, sweet-smelling forehead had a little drop of sweat. How could Harper possibly give her up? But how would they survive? She didn't want to tell the Anderssons that Anna had been born, afraid of the possibility it would open up. Harper knew that other people thought the same way her mother did: it would be best to give Anna up, but Harper couldn't bear to do it.

Part of it, and Harper knew this was silly, was the fact that she wasn't going to college next year anyway. She'd been too pregnant and preoccupied to finish her applications, hadn't had an abortion like a smart, ambitious girl would have. If she gave Anna up, she'd have nothing. Or she'd have her freedom, but it wouldn't be enough.

Mrs. Wood arrived an hour later with a bag full of groceries: eggs, bread, orange juice with calcium, lettuce, milk, butter, muffins and fruit. Harper unpacked the food, relieved to have it, but angry that her own mother hadn't done it.

"This is so nice of you. I'll give you a check," Harper said.

"My dear, I wouldn't think of it. I want to see the baby."

Harper didn't argue. They left the groceries on the counter and went into the living room where Anna lay on a blanket on the floor. Her arms were flung back, next to her head, her pink palms exposed. A tiny red scratch marked her cheek.

Harper bent down to her. "Oh! she scratched her face with her fingernail."

"Babies do that," Mrs. Wood crouched down, her knees cracking. "Harper, she's just beautiful. I want to hold her, but she looks pretty content right now."

"It's okay," Harper said. "Why don't you sit in the recliner and I'll give her to you."

Mrs. Wood stood up slowly, her knees cracking again, and Harper gently lifted Anna up and placed her in Mrs. Wood's arms.

"Oh, she's so light!" Mrs. Wood smiled. "I'll hold her here, while you put those things in the icebox."

Harper smiled. "Hardly anyone says 'ice box' anymore."

"Habit, I suppose. My mother said it."

Harper put the groceries away, mentally adding up what they must have cost, and walked back into the living room. "I really should pay you," she said.

"Absolutely not, but Harper, I must say it's disturbing that your mother would go out and leave you without food."

Harper flopped down on the couch and watched Mrs. Wood holding Anna. "She's trying to make a point," Harper said.

"Which is?"

"That I can't manage on my own. She doesn't want us to stay here. She wants me to give Anna up for adoption."

Mrs. Wood did something with her lips that Harper couldn't quite interpret, then set Anna back down on her blanket. She sat next to Harper on the couch, and Harper giggled. Mrs. Wood looked at her, puzzled.

"It's so funny," Harper said. "We're sitting here, watching her sleep. It's crazy. She can't even speak."

"It doesn't sound like you want to give her up."

"I don't. But my mother keeps telling me it would be best for her, or how am I going to manage, or go to college, and I know she's right. I don't know what's wrong with me, because giving her up should feel like it's getting me off the hook—and it would, a little bit, because I don't know what I'll do for a living. I was planning to figure that out when I went to college." Harper took a deep breath. "You were so nice to give me work at the motel when I was pregnant, but if I come back to work, I'll have to pay someone almost the same amount I'm making, and that doesn't make any sense."

Mrs. Woods gazed down at Anna. "Harper, I wish I had a good answer for you, but I don't. I would say this: if you truly want to keep her, you probably should. I never had children because, oh, I don't know, there didn't seem to be the right person at the right time. By the time I married Bill, he was done raising his family and I was older. But I think it would be difficult to give her up and have that regret."

Mrs. Woods' long face was mournful. Harper imagined that she hadn't been pretty, even when she was young.

"I brought you something." Mrs. Woods reached around the side of the couch and pulled out a shopping bag that said *Motherhood*. She handed Harper a box wrapped in yellow paper.

Harper opened the package to find two loose-fitting shirts, one jade green, one pale blue, made of thick jersey cotton. She ran her hand along the neatly finished seams.

"They're nursing shirts," Mrs. Wood said. "My sister has two little girls, and she says these are really handy. Look . . ." she reached behind a seam that Harper hadn't noticed. "You can nurse Anna without having to pull your whole shirt up. It's easier if you're out in public. No one can even tell you're nursing."

•

WHEN HARPER WOKE in the morning, her breasts full
and aching, she needed Anna to nurse. Harper hated waking
her; it was so rare to have a moment of peace, but finally, when
she couldn't stand it anymore, Anna woke, opened her mouth
to cry, and milk sprouted from Harper's breasts in tiny streams
before Anna even started nursing. Harper usually started on
the left side, her breast hard and swollen, and Anna would
suck intently, her temple pulsing as she drank. Then, Harper's
breast softened, became comfortably depleted, and she'd nurse
Anna on the other side. Anna sometimes fell asleep with her
tiny fingers on Harper's breast.

Symbiosis. A word she'd learned in science class. They
needed each other. Sitting in the corduroy recliner, nursing
Anna, she felt a vast contentment. The delicate outline of
Anna's ear, her smushy nose, her downy eyebrows and pale
brown hair had become embedded in Harper's vision. She felt,
although she knew it didn't really make sense, that she was not
just a girl trapped in an ugly apartment. Somehow, she would
get out of here. Harper touched the star-like lines on Anna's
knuckles. As long as Harper was nursing her, as long as she had
diapers and wipes, a change of clothes, Anna had everything
she needed.

•

DR. WATKINS HAD suggested that taking a bath might be
soothing, but when Harper got into the bathtub and looked
at her stomach, she started to weep. Her skin, loose and baggy, curled in on her belly button like some strange kind of
mushroom. A tawny line ran from her navel down to her pubic
hair, but the line wavered in her soft, rumply flesh. The nurse
had said that breastfeeding Anna would help her get back to
her normal shape, but Harper felt frightened by this rumpled
evidence of her pregnancy.

She slept more lightly now; when Anna cried, Harper woke. She learned to bring her into bed and nurse her. Then they both fell back asleep. In the mornings, her mother dressed, used the bathroom, went to work, and Harper stayed in her bedroom until her mother left. She knew her mother's resentment, but it seemed distant and unimportant once she was gone. Harper looked down at Anna, saw her breathing, touched her moist little fists, then curled around her and went back to sleep.

Anna cried, she nursed her. Anna pooped, she changed her. Anna needed to get outside, Harper took her outdoors. There was no one to talk to, so she read library books while Anna was napping, and talked to her when she was awake. Harper had listened to what Dr. Watkins said and didn't let Anna stay too long in the sun, made sure she had a little hat. When she took her out: to visit at the Motel 6, or to the grocery store, people would look at Anna and say, "What a beautiful baby!" Harper felt a rush of pride.

During the day, when her mother wasn't home, Harper described the world to Anna. *This is the shirt that Mrs. Woods gave me. It feels nice. Katie told me it came from a really expensive store in Cleveland. When I went into labor, Mrs. Woods was there. I didn't know for sure if you'd be a boy or a girl. Can you imagine? I can't wait for you to meet David. He knows Mom is crazy. He gave me a magic charm against her. David goes to school at Madison. I'm going to college, too. I just have to figure out when. I need to finish high school first. I was too pregnant with you, but it won't be hard, I was almost done anyway. Maybe it's better that I'm waiting because it would be good to know what I'm going to college for. Last year, I just wanted to get away, but it's a lot of money to spend, so it would be better to know why I'm going. We are going somewhere. I'm just not sure where. Maybe Washington State. I've never been there, but it's supposed to be pretty. I want you to meet your father.*

She said things that Janet wouldn't understand, or that Katie would override with knowledge of her own. She talked about things David didn't want to hear. Once, when Harper was younger, her father had sent her a diary with a tiny lock and key. The book was thick, with gold on the page edges, and writing in it was like having someone to talk to. Once, she'd left it unlocked in her room, and her mother had come in and read it. Harper had written that she wished her father would visit, other things, too, and her mother had thrown the diary in the dumpster. Harper had pitched an absolute fit, tried to climb into the dumpster, and her mother had yanked her out, banging Harper's arm on the hard metal edge. At the end of it all, she was crying and snotty and confused about what she'd actually done wrong. It was totally unfair. The next day, a huge purple bruise, tinged yellow at the outside, bloomed underneath her arm.

Telling things to Anna, who couldn't repeat them, was safer.

Her mother usually stayed out for happy hour now, and mostly, Harper wished she wouldn't come home. When she came home late, she smoked in the apartment; she smoked inside when it was raining. Harper tried, one night, to remind her what Dr. Watkins had said, but her mother looked at her with contempt.

"You get yourself knocked up at seventeen, and you ask me not to smoke in my own place? You've got to be kidding."

"I know you're mad about Anna, but you barely buy food! Legally, you're supposed to feed me until I'm eighteen. The least you could do is smoke outside."

Her mother glared and struck another match.

•

HARPER KEPT THE car seat in the apartment so Anna could sit up and see her as she washed dishes or moved around, cleaning up. When Harper needed to shower, she'd haul the car seat into the bathroom and peek out of the shower curtain so Anna would know she was there.

High school graduation was coming up, and Harper debated about whether to go. Matt was class valedictorian, and when Katie reported he was going to Dartmouth, Harper's stomach dropped. The concreteness of the fact made her own life seem foolish. Katie and Janet had both been noticeably circumspect about graduation and beyond, but Katie, it turned out, was going to Bowling Green State in the fall, and Janet had signed up for nursing classes at the community college. Harper knew they didn't discuss their plans because they didn't want her to feel bad.

The triangle of their friendship had shifted. Before, Harper had been the glue between Katie and Janet, who both liked her, but didn't have much in common. Now, as they started to move ahead in their lives, Harper imagined they were united by feeling sorry for her.

Harper got dressed that Saturday morning as if it were possible that she might see her friends graduate. When she walked into to kitchen, her mother was mixing a Bloody Mary.

"Morning," Harper said, and went to the refrigerator for some orange juice. Her mother would take this as a rebuke, but she didn't know what else to do. She carried her glass back into the living room, and her mother followed her.

"So, all dressed up and nowhere to go?"

Harper lifted Anna onto the couch and propped her between two cushions. "What are you planning to do?"

"I haven't figured that out yet."

"You think you can just lie around here and sleep and eat while I go out and work?"

"No, but Anna is still little. Who else is going to feed her? You said yourself that formula is expensive."

"If you think, after raising you and David, that I'm going to support you all over again, through raising another kid, you've got another think coming."

"Okay! I've heard this before. I really am trying to think of something."

"You've always made it so damn clear that you wanted to get out. Why would you want to raise a kid here? You should give the baby to those people who can actually do something for it, and go to school like you planned."

Harper turned to look at Anna, who stared at her mother as if mesmerized. Anna looked down towards her foot, then wobbled a plump little fist.

14

THE SUMMER STRETCHED in front of her. Hours and days of intense boredom. She'd felt this way last summer, but there was a sense of possibility then. Now, there was nothing. If she lived somewhere different, she could put Anna in a stroller, go window-shopping, eat ice cream, but there was none of that around here. Still, she had the necessities: a roof over her head, her mother at work all day, an air conditioner when it got too hot. And really, much of the day was taken up with feeding Anna, changing her, watching her.

All Anna wanted was to be held and nursed, held and nursed, and even though Harper was tired, she liked being able to comfort her. She looked at the clock and sighed, 9:37 A.M. How was she going to get through the day? If she had just one activity planned, it made the day bearable. Mrs. Wood had come by a few times to take Harper and Anna to the library. She also told Harper that she could come over and swim whenever she liked, so a few days a week, Harper packed diapers, wipes, and a towel in her backpack, gathered up Anna, and carried her in the car seat, which was heavy, through the trailer park and over to the Motel 6. Harper's arms had grown strong, but it was tiring, lugging the car seat. Still, she couldn't simply lay Anna on the cement at the pool. Even with baby blankets, it didn't seem right. Today, since it was already humid, Harper decided to go for a swim.

As she carried Anna, the car seat, and the diaper bag, she felt sweat trickle down her back. The frog lady was out tending her garden, although Harper could see little evidence of anything growing. She set Anna and the car seat down next to the garden plot, just to catch her breath.

"Well, the spinach is coming," the woman said.

"Where?" Harper asked.

"Right there."

Harper bent down and peered into the dirt. She didn't see anything—was the woman just pretending?—then saw three rows of tiny two-leaved plants; they couldn't have been more than half-an-inch tall.

"That's great." Harper felt as if she were talking to a child, pretending she understood something incomprehensible. She picked up Anna in the car seat. "Thanks for showing me. I'll see you on my way back."

The pool was small, but clean, and during the week, hardly anyone used it. She set Anna in the shade, close enough to the pool so Anna could see her. Then Harper dove in, felt the cool water close over her. She played peekaboo with Anna, plunging down into the water, bright aquamarine around her, then up, a silvery jack-in-the-box. Harper had gotten the tiniest of smiles from her, but Anna hadn't really giggled yet. Harper wanted to hear what her laugh would be like. It would be an important first thing, like rolling over, or her first steps. Her first laugh. Anna watched her, and seemed to take Harper's submersion and reappearance in stride.

•

A FEW WEEKS after graduation, Katie called and asked Harper over. That morning, as she dressed Anna, Harper made sure Anna was wearing a onesie that Mrs. Gallagher had given her.

When Katie came to pick her up, they got the car seat strapped into the back, then buckled Anna in. Katie started the car then turned off the radio.

"You don't call us anymore."

Her matter-of-fact tone startled Harper. Clearly, there was a point to this visit.

"I'm not much fun these days." Harper looked out the window. She didn't want to be clutchy, prove her mother right, when the need was so clearly on her side.

"How much fun is there around here anyway? You're fine. My mother's dying to see Anna."

When they walked into the house, the light-colored carpet, the glass candy dishes, the bay window filled with plants, seemed like decorations from a different world. Mrs. Gallagher hurried over to see Anna. "Oh Harper, she's just adorable. Katie said you did a great job with the birth."

"I don't know about great job, but I couldn't have really imagined it."

Katie's younger brother loped into the kitchen, took a banana off the counter, glanced at the baby, and went to refrigerator.

"Say hello, Kevin."

"Hello, Kevin."

Mrs. Gallagher rolled her eyes, and for a moment, Harper could imagine her as a teenager herself. "Don't get snotty with me. Please mow the lawn before you leave with Philip."

"Got it, Mom." He glanced at Anna. "Pretty cute," he said.

Mrs. Gallagher poured iced tea for Harper and Katie. "Let's sit out back in the shade," she said. "I want to look out on my garden."

Harper carried Anna outside. The backyard did look nice: mulched borders punctuated by broad, leafy plants and bright azaleas; clearly Mrs. Gallagher had been busy. White wicker furniture faced the lawn, like a picture in a magazine.

She gestured that Harper should sit down, and set an iced tea on a little table next to her.

The chairs looked pretty, but when Harper sat down, the wicker strands dug into her back.

Mrs. Gallagher smiled at Anna and ran her fingers over Anna's hands. Anna gazed at her solemnly. "She's just adorable, Harper. I'm glad you're keeping her. I think it's good. It might not seem smart, but it's good."

"You're one of the only people to say that," Harper said. She shifted Anna to her other arm, so her face wouldn't be in the sun, and reached for her tea.

Mrs. Gallagher stirred the ice cubes in her tea with her finger, then licked it. "Katie says your mom still hasn't warmed up about it."

"She keeps saying that she just got done raising me, and she doesn't want to do it all over again. I do get her point. I just have to figure out what I'm going to do."

Mrs. Gallagher pursed her lips. "Well, it's not for me to say, but your mother could be a bit more sympathetic. She got pregnant with your brother at the end of high school, or at least that's what we all guessed, given the quick wedding, and your brother's birthday and all."

Harper felt a thrum of surprise, a quickening in her stomach.

"Oh!" Mrs. Gallagher's cheeks quivered. She looked down and made a little swirling motion with her glass. Harper could see she'd meant to show she was in on the secret, which she now realized Harper didn't know. Katie flushed. Her mother must have already said something to her.

"My mother doesn't say much about my dad, so I don't know my parents' anniversary." She thought of David's birthday, January 12, and mentally counted backward.

"I shouldn't have opened my mouth." Mrs. Gallagher's expression was apologetic, but she didn't sound particularly sorry.

"No, I'm glad you did. My mother won't tell me anything."

"Well, your father was a nice boy, or I thought so, but we were all just kids then." Mrs. Gallagher studied the backyard, as if eyeing it for her next project, then turned her attention back to Harper. "I don't know that your mother ever planned to go off to college, but I never got the idea that your father planned to stay in Milan. He moved here in high school, as I recall.

Actually, he moved here with another family. They lived outside of town; I didn't really know them. They had a boy, too. What was his name? I'd remember if I heard it. I never quite knew what the story was, but your father and his friend, they were always together, two peas in a pod. I don't know why your father was living with this family, but then later, after he and your mom got married, the three of them still hung around a lot."

"What happened to his friend?"

"Killed in a car wreck. I saw your dad a day or two after the accident. He was real upset. Both him and your mom. This was a couple years after high school, but it seemed like your dad was never quite the same after that. I have to say, I never really took to your mother, but she wasn't always like she is now."

"My mom won't talk about him at all."

"Is your dad in touch with you?"

"Not really. A birthday card, sometimes, you know."

•

HARPER HOPED THAT her mother would grow accustomed to Anna, but her mother smoked inside more often, barely bought groceries, or bought the absolute minimum. She made Harper pay for diapers out of her savings, which Harper supposed was fair, but she made Harper give her a check each time, as if she didn't trust her. Once, she took a blank check and made it out for ten dollars over—to cover gas, she said. After that, Harper went with her. In the drugstore, her mother walked by the display for baby formula, commenting, "Better hope your milk doesn't dry up. This stuff costs a fortune."

•

AT NIGHT, ANNA cried to be nursed, and mostly Harper's mother slept through it, although occasionally Anna woke her, and then her mother yelled, Anna wailed, and Harper tried to calm them both down. Once, Harper dreamed her mother stole Anna and sold her to someone while Harper was at work. Harper woke, her breasts leaking, heart pounding. Anna slept next to her, a solid, sweet-smelling lump.

By the time Anna was six weeks old, Harper's mother grew quiet, and Harper wasn't sure if her silence was brooding or accepting. One night, her mother came home and made hamburgers for dinner. She set a plate in front of Harper, who squeezed a huge amount of ketchup onto her burger. Anna was napping, and Harper wanted to eat before Anna woke up.

"Of course," her mother said. "If the county found you unfit, they'd take Anna away. They'd put her in foster care."

Harper set the bun back on her burger and looked up. "What do you mean 'unfit'?"

"Getting pregnant at a rave, where people are doing drugs."

Harper took a bite of hamburger, chewed and swallowed. Inside, she was trembling, but knew she couldn't show it. "I didn't go to a rave. I wasn't doing any drugs."

"Be tough for you to prove now, wouldn't it?"

Harper heard Anna stirring and got up to see if she was really awake. Her diaper was heavy, and Harper changed her, brought her to the table, and nursed her while she nibbled on her meal. She ate her burger and stared her mother down: she and Anna on one end of the table, her mother on the other, like an uneven see-saw. Finally, her mother grabbed her purse and walked out, slapping the screen door behind her.

Harper finished dinner, then, carrying Anna, she sat down on the couch and looked out the window. At the end of June, the trees thick and full, the air balmy, she wished she could feel happy. It was a time to be outdoors, to go somewhere fun, to be with people who made you laugh. She imagined Nate lived in a world where people got together for meals, went hiking or camping, had parties outside, bonfires at night. There must be a place where she could have a different kind of life. Would her mother really try to say she was unfit? How did her mother know about a rave that had happened almost a year ago?

The next day, when Harper went to the Motel 6 to swim, she picked up a copy of the local newspaper. There was a story about a building in Sandusky that had been closed down after a series of raves. It wasn't the first article on the story. Her mother must have read the articles, fished for information, and guessed at what she couldn't figure out.

•

ON WEEKENDS, WHEN her mother was home, Harper retreated to her bedroom. She sifted through what she thought of as her life: kid stuff, letters from David, birthday cards from her father. A little desk had come with the apartment, and she used it for school books, paper, pens and pencils, an electric pencil sharpener that was a gift from her father. He'd sent it when she was eight. She used to send him long letters with houses drawn on them, pictures of her waving to him. She'd thought an electric pencil sharpener was the coolest thing ever: black and shiny, rectangular, a hole on the end, surrounded by chrome. She loved pushing the pencils in, the electric whir of resistance, having them come out sharp and smelling of fresh wood. Shortly after her father sent it, Harper overheard her mother talking to someone on the phone. "A pencil sharpener. A fucking electric pencil sharpener. He probably stole it."

Harper pressed a dull pencil into it, listened to it whir, and ground the pencil down to a fine, sharp point.

·

HARPER FELT HER heart pounding. She was running, running in her dream. Anna was screaming, shrieking, and Harper ran to her bedroom door. The door of bedroom was locked, and Harper pulled on the door, pulled and pulled, heard Anna screaming, and finally she yanked the door open and ran into the room. Her mother was holding Anna on the desk, pressing Anna's fingers into the electric pencil sharpener. Anna was on her back on the desk and her mother leaned over her, pressing the soft flesh of her fingers, one by one, into the little hole. Anna's screaming shattered her dream. Harper woke, sweating, her heart thudding. Anna was in her little drawer on the floor, yelling like she'd never yelled before. Oh God, oh God, oh God, Harper slapped on the light to see Anna's fingers, scoop her up. Her fingers were whole, pink and unharmed.

Harper picked her up, put the tips of Anna's fingers in her mouth, held them against her tongue, but Anna was still screaming. She lowered Anna to her breast.

Blood throbbed in her head. The dream was a warning.

She nursed Anna for a long time, with the light on, so the dream wouldn't come back. Anna hiccupped, then settled. It took Harper hours to get back to sleep. She kept Anna in bed with her, and all the next day, Harper felt edgy and sad, the dream like a shadow in the corner of her vision. She tried to shake it off by taking care of chores. She washed all her laundry and Anna's. She folded their clothes, put them away, then went for a swim, carrying Anna in her car seat over to the Motel 6.

As Harper carried Anna through the trailer park, she nodded to the frog lady, but didn't have the energy for another strange conversation.

Harper told herself it was just a bad dream. Maybe Anna had gotten a tiny splinter. Maybe, when Harper put Anna's fingers in her mouth, it had come out. Harper didn't want to tell anyone about the dream, but it seemed as real to her as if something had happened. Would her mother really try to show she was unfit? Harper was afraid that, if a social worker did question her, if she were forced to tell the name of Anna's father to someone official, she'd have to reveal that she'd slept with someone who'd been in town for a few days, whose last name she didn't know. The bare facts seemed cheap.

After swimming, Harper lay on the warm cement and looked past Anna, toward the freeway. She had always hoped that, deep down, her mother wanted to be a better person, wanted to be more like what a mother should be. But in the past weeks, especially when her mother didn't buy food, Harper started to think that she'd to have choose between hope and practicality. Her dream pressed her to admit it—her mother wasn't going to change. She couldn't keep hoping and keep Anna safe. She had to get out of here.

Her mother wasn't above lying, and the more Harper thought about this, the more it frightened her. When her mother didn't come home that evening, Harper sat out on the cement deck with Anna and tried to think—about Nate, about everything. What should she do? She felt as if she were trying to squeeze mud through a pastry tube; she couldn't imagine her next step.

Anna was wakeful that night, nursing more frequently than usual. Harper slept lightly, and it seemed that the only real sleep she got was early in the morning, after her mother left for work.

When Harper finally woke in the mid-morning heat, heavy-headed and dull, she walked into the living room to see what the weather looked like. The light on the phone machine flickered. One message. Harper hit the button.

"This is Henry Jacobsen from Sandusky County Social Services returning a call. You had concerns about the safety of an infant? Something about an infant being left alone in a hot car? Please call me back as soon as possible at......"

Harper stared at the machine and started to tremble. She played the message again. "Oh God, oh God, oh God," Harper murmured. Her mother would get Anna taken away.

Adrenaline thrummed through her. She wanted to go over to the Motel 6 to get Katie, to ask her advice, maybe talk to Katie's mother. She caught a glimpse of herself in the mirror— her hair greasy, her face creased from sleep. Harper took the fastest shower of her life, dressed, slipped Anna into the Snugli, and half-walked, half-ran over to the motel, cupping the back of Anna's head so she wouldn't bounce too much. When Harper burst in, Katie was checking in two families. A tall, angular woman was insisting on another room. By her aggrieved tone, the jut of her hip, it was clear that the woman would not be easily appeased. Katie's cheeks were flushed, her mouth open, as she tried to pacify the woman. Harper felt frantic, like a dog in a pen, or a child who has to pee. Mrs. Wood was off today. Katie was too busy to be interrupted. Harper hurried outside with Anna and turned back toward the apartment.

In the trailer park, the frog lady was sitting in a lawn chair, gazing at her garden.

Harper smiled politely and edged between the woman's garden and the next trailer. She had to get home and think.

"My son's been visiting me."

"That's nice," Harper said.

"He's on his way to Portland. A land of growing things."

Portland. Was that Washington? Oregon. Harper stopped. "Do you think he'd give me a ride?"

"With your baby?"

"Yes, of course."

The woman squinted. Her wide mouth had a thin-lipped, dazed half-smile. Harper imagined a long tongue shooting out of her mouth.

"I don't know," the woman said. "You'd have to ask him."

"When's he coming?"

"Should be here in a little while. I'm making egg salad."

Anna started to fuss in her Snugli. Harper hurried home, set Anna down, and called Janet. "Janet, I need a favor. Can you run me to the bank?"

"I've got to take a shower before going to work."

"It's really, really important."

Janet sighed, "Okay, but be ready. I'll come up and get you. I don't want to be late."

Anna cried; she wanted to nurse. How to get everything done? Harper carried the car seat down to the curb of the parking lot, then came back for her purse and Anna. She sat on the curb and let Anna nurse. When Janet pulled up, Anna wasn't done, but there wasn't time to wait.

Harper stuck her finger in the side of Anna's mouth and popped her off her breast. Anna started to fuss. Harper told her "more later," but of course, Anna didn't understand. Harper handed Anna to Janet, then set the car seat in the back, fumbling with the straps as she tried to fasten it quickly.

Anna cried and Janet made silly faces to distract her, but it worked only momentarily.

They all got into the car, and Harper hoped the ride would make Anna fall asleep.

"You're not planning to rob the bank, are you?" Janet smiled, then pulled out of the parking lot.

"I've got to leave."

"What?"

"My mom called Social Services. She's trying to have Anna taken away."

Janet glanced at Harper, then turned back to the road. "What are you talking about?"

"She's been threatening it. Saying she can prove me unfit. And you know the crazy frog lady—the one by the Motel 6?"

"Yeah?"

"Her son is passing through town; he's driving to Portland. I'm going to ask him for a ride. I've got to get out of here. I think . . . look, you can't say this to anyone, but I've been dreaming that my mother hurts Anna. Really hurts her. I think she could do that, and then say it was me. I can't stay here."

Janet pulled up to the bank's drive-in window. Anna wailed in the back, and Harper found it hard to concentrate, as if Anna's crying was a wall she couldn't see beyond. Focus, she told herself. She knew her balance: $834.42. She took out everything except for $20.

"How do you want it?" the teller asked.

Harper was confused. She looked at Janet.

"She means, 'What kind of bills?'"

"Oh," Harper thought for a minute. "Twenties and fifties."

"Do you think it's a good idea to ask some guy you don't know for a ride?"

"Probably not, but I've got to get out of here, and this might be my chance. If we stop at a motel, I've got money for my own room. Listen, Janet, this is really important—they'll figure out I took money out of the bank, but if anyone asks where I've gone, tell them I went East—to Cleveland or Columbus. I've basically got to stay away until I turn eighteen. It's only about a month from now. Once I turn eighteen, my mother can't make me come back."

Janet's eyes filled with tears. "I can't believe you're doing this. It feels really serious. More serious than being pregnant."

Harper was holding more money than she'd ever had in her life. She put $334 and change in her purse, then folded the other $500 in her hand. When Janet stopped back at the apartment, Harper got out, went to the back seat, and before getting a hiccuping Anna out, she slipped the money between the lining of the car seat and the hard plastic base. No one would find it there. She'd noticed already that men tended to avoid babies' butts.

Harper handed Anna to Janet, unhooked the car seat, and set it on the curb.

"Listen, I don't have much time, I have to run in and pack." Harper took Anna from Janet, who chewed on her lip. A red barrette, shaped like a bow, slipped down her hair.

"I'm scared for you," Janet said. "When you get to a place where it's safe, call my cell."

"I'll try." Harper shifted Anna on her hip and hugged Janet with the other arm. "Okay, I've got to go. Thanks for the ride, I hope you're not late for work."

It wasn't the right kind of good-bye, and as Janet pulled out of the parking lot, Harper wanted to cry, run after her, but Anna started squalling. "Okay, okay," Harper muttered. "Just give me a chance to get in the door." She lugged the car seat up the steps, and then sat down in the living room, trying to think as Anna nursed. Oh, she was thirsty. She wasn't thirsty before. It was always right as she sat down to nurse Anna. She didn't want to get up for something to drink now, so she tried to think about what she could take—the diaper bag, fill it with baby clothes, diapers, and wipes. She should pack the Snugli, bring two little hats, since Anna tended to knock them off her head. That was all Anna needed, really. Harper would take her backpack, which was all she could manage with Anna and the diaper bag. She wished she had a stroller, but it wouldn't make things any easier at the moment. When Anna was done, Harper dumped the contents of her purse into the front pouch of her backpack. The morning had been cool, and she put on a sweatshirt and a pair of jeans, figuring heavy clothes were easier to wear than to pack. She packed shorts, her other nursing top, three T-shirts, two bras, several pairs of underwear and socks. She glanced at the clock. 12:10.

Anna lay on her back on Harper's bed. At seven weeks old she was plumping up. She looked peaceful and happy, waving her little hands. You have no idea what's going on, Harper thought. She snapped on the Snugli and lifted Anna up, then down into it. It was hard to hold Anna and guide her legs through the holes. If Anna kicked or wriggled, she'd end up sitting on her own leg, bending it awkwardly. Harper leaned Anna on her shoulder, holding her with one hand, making sure both of her legs went through the holes with her other hand. Oh! It would be so much easier if there was someone around to help with the smallest things: when she'd just sat down and needed a glass of water, when she needed someone to hold Anna for a minute. Her mother would sometimes watch her struggle without offering to help. When Harper glanced up, her mother's expression was malicious and satisfied, as if to say, this is your own fault, deal with it yourself.

Before walking out the door, Harper brushed her hair and quickly put some eyeliner around her eyes.

When she got to the frog lady's trailer, a blue Buick sedan was pulled up on the grass. The frog lady sat in her lawn chair, drinking iced tea with an unshaven man who looked to be somewhere in his early thirties.

"This is my son, Caleb," she said. Caleb nodded.

"Did your mother tell you I have a favor to ask?"

"You look like that singer, the one who has a video on

MTV. What's her name?"

Harper brushed a hand in front of her face, as if this were an annoyance, like a fly. "Yeah, I know, people say that."

He took a bite of egg salad sandwich with his mouth already full. "What's the favor?"

"I'm looking for a ride out west."

"I'll give you a ride."

"I'm bringing my baby." Harper brushed away a mosquito that buzzed near Anna's shoulder, then looked at him, wide-eyed, and kissed the top of Anna's head.

"Oh," he reached up to scratch under the band of a DeKalb feed cap, tilting it to the side. "I don't know about a baby."

"If we stop at a motel, I can pay for my own room."

"I was planning to drive straight through, much as I can. I don't know about a baby, though."

"She's really good."

"Well, I was going to have some lunch here and then go on."

"I'm all packed. I can give you some money for gas."

He looked at her, suspicious, then glanced at his car, as if trying to decide whether she would fit. "I can't take lots of junk."

"My backpack and a diaper bag, that's it."

Anna was sleeping, tucked against Harper's chest, her fist curled under her chin. Harper rested her hand on Anna's head. "She sleeps all the time. See how quiet she is? She won't be any trouble." Harper tried to smile, to give the appearance of being calm. Inside, she felt as if she were screaming. The man gazed at her, and Harper looked back at him, fierce, willing him to say 'yes.'

"Okay," he said. "I'm leaving soon, though."

"I'm ready," she said. "You can eat your lunch, and she can nap until it's time to go. See that apartment building, right over there? I live in apartment 21. Just come over when you're done."

He nodded. The frog mother watched them both, benign.

Harper was shaking as she carried Anna back home.
She hated to disturb her by taking her out of the Snugli, but
thought it would be good for her to stretch out, since she'd be
sitting in the car for so long. Harper laid her in her little drawer
bed and looked around the room at the dust motes floating in
light. This was the last time she'd see this place. Anna wouldn't
even remember it.

She tried to think of anything else she might need: David's
address and phone number; Katie's and Janet's she knew by
heart. Reaching into her nightstand, she took Anna's birth
certificate, her immunization records. She took the envelope
that held her father's last birthday card, his return address in
La Crosse scribbled in the corner. Harper surveyed her posters, which had meant little anyway, her schoolbooks, her notes.
Should she leave her mother a note? She pulled a piece of paper from a spiral notebook. She wanted to write something that
would shut her mother up, force her not to look for her. She
thought of the night her mother had wanted her to do karaoke,
the thousand times her mother had told her how stupid she
was. The pen would press the paper and say nothing.

Mom—
> *Bye,*
>> *Harper*

Outside, a horn honked. The Buick pulled up in the parking lot. Anna was still sleeping, so Harper put her backpack on,
slung the diaper bag over her shoulder, and carried the car seat
downstairs. Caleb opened the back door. There was no seatbelt
in the middle of the back seat, which was littered with candy wrappers and bags from fast food places. She brushed the

wrappers off the seat and put the car seat behind the driver's side so she could easily glance over and see Anna. Something sticky from the wrappers stuck to her hand, and she tried not to make a face. Her mother wasn't due home for hours. Had she given Social Services their address? *Get out of here, get out of here* banged in her head. She strapped the car seat in tightly, put the diaper bag and backpack on the back seat, then told him, "I'll just get Anna. I'll be back in a minute." She ran up the stairs, washed her hands quickly, then lifted Anna out of the drawer, pulling the blanket out with her, hoping she'd stay asleep. Her heart hammered as if she were being chased. She felt for money in her pocket, remembered her backpack and the money in the car seat, then closed the apartment door behind her.

Gently, she set Anna into her car seat, fastened the clips, but the movement woke her up and Anna squawked in protest.

"She'll settle as soon as we get going," Harper said, and climbed in front. Caleb looked at her doubtfully, then pulled out of the parking lot.

For the first few minutes Anna was quiet, but after her nap she was hungry and started to fuss. Harper tried a pacifier, tried dangling a toy in front of her.

"This isn't going to work," he said. He glanced in the rear-view mirror, then looked over at Harper.

"Let's just stop for a second. I can nurse her."

"I'll get gas." Caleb's voice was flat.

Anna started to cry, picking up volume, and Harper scanned the horizon for gas stations. She dangled her keys in front of Anna and made little cooing noises. Inside, she was pleading, *please stop, please stop.*

He turned off at a truckstop, and Harper quickly got into the backseat and nursed Anna as he put gas in the car. He seemed embarrassed that she was nursing a baby, and tugged on the bill of his cap, didn't look in the back window or ask if she wanted anything before heading inside.

She was thirsty, dying for something to drink, but it was too late to say so now. She didn't want to make him wait. He was weird—but who cared?—not scary weird, just sort of gross. He came back with a Big Gulp and a long piece of beef jerky, which Harper could smell from the back seat. She wanted to make sure Anna got enough, so she wouldn't fuss, but Harper knew that he wouldn't want to stand around, waiting. *Please finish, please finish*, Harper thought. Anna paused for a moment in her sucking, and Harper hoped it would be enough. She picked her up, brought her own nose up against Anna's, then kissed her neck. Anna seemed happy. Harper clipped her into the car seat, and they set out again.

There was little to see in Northern Ohio—green and white highway signs pointing to little towns, places no one wanted to stop. On the road ahead, a dark shimmering on the horizon, like water in the distance, wavered and receded before them. Harper took a deep breath and let it out slowly. She was getting away. She would do it! Everything was wide and open in front of her. It would cost money to get from Portland to Olympia. Maybe she could take a bus or a train; she could rent a little apartment for her and Anna. What would it cost? She wasn't sure. Maybe she could get a job like that woman in the antiques store who had her baby with her. A little doubt whispered: people won't hire you if you have a baby. She pushed the thought back down.

She would go to Olympia, run into Nate, and it would probably be awkward at first. He would look at her and realize he had missed her. What would she say? "Surprise! See, I did come out to see what this place was like." He would look at Anna and wonder. She would say, "Let's have a talk," and tell him quietly that Anna was his daughter. If, the first time she saw him again, he was with Paco or other friends, it would be weird. What if he had a girlfriend?

Her stomach clutched. She hadn't imagined it until now, but what if he did? He wasn't the type to just be with someone lightly, was he? It didn't seem like it, but look what had happened to her. What would she do if he had a girlfriend? The fact that she'd overlooked this possibility frightened her.

They drove through Toledo. Caleb didn't require conversation. He listened to country music and tapped his fingers on the steering wheel. The car grew warm; Harper wished she had a 7UP, something bubbly and sweet. The car didn't have air conditioning, and he opened his window wide as they sped down the highway. Anna started to cry again. Caleb cursed under his breath and turned the music up. Harper guessed the wind was bothering her. She couldn't ask him to roll up his window; maybe she could put the car seat behind her, so she could leave her window up and it wouldn't blow on Anna so much. Anna started to wail, and he glanced over at Harper. They were several hours out now, and she couldn't tell if he was a little annoyed, or really annoyed. He nodded toward a sign for a rest stop, then pulled into the right lane, heading for it. Harper felt a vast relief.

"You take her in and change her. Do whatever you need to do to get her to stop crying."

"It's probably just the wind bothering her. I'll move the car seat behind me when I come back."

He parked in the side parking lot, and she got out, stepping into the heat rising off the pavement. Her sweaty clothes stuck to her. She pulled the diaper bag out of the car.

"Do we have time for me to change into shorts and a T-shirt?"

"Take all the time you need." Caleb studied her and scratched under his headband.

She put her backpack squarely on her back and set the

diaper bag on the pavement. Then she unclipped Anna, picking
her up so she could lean against her chest, and threw the diaper
bag over her other shoulder. The bag was heavy with Anna's
clothes and diapers.

"I'll be out in a little bit."

He nodded, gazing straight ahead.

Harper walked into the rest stop, and the clean, cool of air
conditioning washed over her.

She smelled coffee, sugar, soy sauce. Oh, she was starving
and thirsty. Ohio had these really nice rest stops, light and airy,
all along the turnpike. The food court had a TCBY, Starbucks,
and Chinese food. They kept the eating areas clean. She'd get
food when she came out. She went into the ladies' room, where
they had a plastic changing table she could pull down; it had a
little dip in it, so a baby was less likely to roll off. She changed
Anna, who was only a little wet, not enough to be crying, but
Harper didn't want to give her any reason to start crying again.
She wanted to change her own clothes to something cooler,
and wondered how to manage. She couldn't go into a stall;
there was no place to set Anna, and she couldn't leave her out
here, because she didn't want to take a chance on Anna rolling
off the changing table. She wasn't turning over yet, but there
was always a first time. Harper set her backpack on the floor.
She'd just have to change out here, hope no one would come in.
She wriggled out of her jeans and quickly put on shorts, pulled
off her shirt and sweat shirt and put on a tank top. Putting the
bigger clothes in her pack made it bulge dangerously; she didn't
want to break the zippers, but she couldn't help it right now.

Peeing was the hardest thing. She carried Anna into the
stall, undid her shorts with one hand, shimmied the shorts
down, thank God they actually had toilet seat covers, peed
while holding the baby, wiped herself awkwardly, God, what
a pain it all was. Just to have someone to hold Anna while

Harper used the bathroom would make life so much easier. Anna squirmed in her arms, and Harper set her back on the changing table so she could get her shorts zipped up.

The whole process seemed to take forever, but Anna seemed happier and, since there was no one around, Harper kept up a little running talk with her. In the car with Caleb, she couldn't talk to Anna the way she usually did, and it made her aware of how much time she spent talking to her daughter, keeping up a little stream of explanations. This is how we put on your shirt, Katie's mother said that everyone has onesies. Did you know you were outgrowing your little drawer? You were right next to my bed, and I liked having you there. Don't listen to your grandma, she's a crabby pants and she doesn't know what she's talking about. You have an Uncle David, who's going to meet you and think you're the cutest thing he's ever seen. Harper hadn't quite understood how lonely she'd been before Anna was born, and now that she was here, Harper had an audience for all the things she thought about. She'd told Anna about Mr. Silvano, her Earth Science teacher, how earnest he was, how she thought he was kind of cute. She told her that she wanted to live somewhere clean and pretty. She told her about the Anderssons, and how nice they were, but how she couldn't bear to let Anna go live with them.

Harper put on her backpack, slung the diaper bag over her shoulder, picked Anna up, and headed out of the ladies' room. The smell of egg rolls made her hungry, but it was too hot to eat them, maybe frozen yogurt, she wanted one, but she couldn't manage one more thing in her hands, the diaper bag only barely staying on her shoulder, so she'd get Anna into the car first and then ask Caleb if he wanted something to make up for the trouble of stopping.

Harper went to the side door she'd come in and scanned the parking lot. She didn't see the Buick. She looked again.

Maybe he couldn't find a parking space, but there were plenty of empty spaces. Maybe he'd gotten gas, or went to clean his windshield. She sighed, hiked her bag up on her shoulder, and walked across the eating area—God, she was wobbly with hunger and thirst—and out the front door to where the gas was. She looked over the islands and didn't see the car. Where could he be? Did he park on the other side? Maybe she'd gotten the entrances confused. The building was shell-shaped, the wide curve facing the highway; maybe she'd gotten turned around. Harper walked toward the other entrance, maybe he'd parked on the other side because he wanted something to eat himself. She looked carefully. No, she didn't see him. Was she misremembering the car? She felt herself shaking. He couldn't have left. Anna started to fuss. He must be getting something to eat. Harper hurried over to the food court, the diaper bag banging on her hip, and looked in all the lines. It wasn't crowded; she didn't see him. She surveyed the tables, looking for his DeKalb feed cap. Where was he? He must be in one of the other lines. She hurried past the Starbucks, her pack heavy, the diaper bag slipping off her shoulder, cupping the back of Anna's head as she moved more quickly: Chinese food, fried chicken, TCBY. She didn't see him anywhere. He could be in the men's room, but if he was, his car would be here. She ran to the other door. Where was the car? She looked in the first parking lot. Nothing. Tears started in her throat. It couldn't be. Her breath was coming hot and hard. She went and stood outside the men's room until a teen-aged boy came out.

"Excuse me, did you see a man in there? A man in a feed cap?"

The boy, greasy-haired, with pimples, looked embarrassed and shook his head.

She waited a few minutes. Maybe he was in a stall, maybe he'd come out, and she stood outside the men's room, her breath jagged in her chest. Even if he was taking a long time, she'd been in the bathroom a long time as well, changing Anna's diaper and her own clothes. He wouldn't still be in there.

She ran back to the first parking lot. He'd be there, he'd have to be, they were just missing each other. She looked again, no. She went to look out the front door, to the gas islands, no. She ran to the other side door, feeling like a rat in a maze. No. All she could see was the turnpike with cars speeding past. She stood in the foyer, looking out at the highway, as it finally sank in. He had left her! He had left! He had left with her car seat. And then a fearful flush rose up in her. Her money! She had tucked $500 into the car seat because she was sure no one would bother it there. He had left her and taken the car seat and most of her money as well.

Harper sank down on her haunches, leaning against a wall with Anna against her chest.

She began to sob. People hurried past. Sneakers, heels, business shoes strode by. Families edged around her. She howled with anger. Nobody stopped to ask her what was wrong.

15

BY 10 O'CLOCK THAT night, Harper felt as if she had shifted into some place she hadn't known existed in herself. The day had become distended; it seemed impossible she'd only left home that morning. When she broke down in the rest stop entrance, Anna started crying as well, and Harper realized, as people scurried around them, that it was dangerous to draw attention to herself. She picked up her bags and carried them to a quiet spot in the eating area. At the food court, she bought eggrolls and juice, carried them to her table, and tried to calm down and think of what to do. The eggrolls were crunchy and greasy and perfect. She wanted a pyramid of them—she would dip them in soy sauce and sweet sauce and mustard; she would eat and eat. It was hard not to burn her mouth. She ate with one hand, Anna resting in her left arm, and studied the people around her. As the food settled in her, she felt calmer, calculating; whether she used sympathy or trickery, she had to get someone to give her a ride.

With Anna in the Snugli, she'd lugged her diaper bag and backpack into the bathroom, washed her face and combed her hair, tried to look less desperate. She walked out to the edge of the tarmac and watched people filling their gas tanks. After Caleb, she didn't want to ask any men for rides. She started to approach two different families for rides, but realized, even before she opened her mouth, that their instinct would probably be to call the police, not take her with them. And not having a car seat—who would take a chance on that?

Behind the rest stop was an empty parking lot backed by a scrubby plot of grass and weeds. A row of saplings tilted in the breeze. The plot ran into a gully, a wire fence, and beyond it lay a huge field covered with acres of a dense green crop, soybeans maybe. There was nothing to hide behind, no shelter. The openness of the pale sky was oppressive. Through the afternoon, when she'd been in the food court too long, or was worried about being too noticeable out on the tarmac, watching for likely rides, she'd retreated here, hoping none of the food service workers would notice her when they came out to put trash in the dumpsters or flatten cardboard for recycling. With Anna in her arms, Harper sat at the border of the scrubby break in the field, and wondered what to do. She couldn't call Katie or Janet, couldn't go back. She wanted to call the Anderssons, but they would only come and get her if she'd give them Anna. She had to get a ride, but how? Who?

Toward the end of the day, she walked around the side parking lot and looked for teenagers, or people in their twenties who might not ask too many questions. Heat rose up from the pavement, and she shifted Anna from arm to arm. Anyone paying attention would notice that she'd been here for hours. She'd tried for rides five times: a single woman, two girls together, a young couple, another set of girls, and two young men who seemed pretty harmless. Each time she approached, with Anna on her hip, and asked if she could get a ride, they had looked at her as if she wasn't speaking English. "What?" they said.

And she asked again. She tried to be brief and vague, simply saying that her ride had left without her. She made it sound as if she'd been on a bus, a tour, that it was a bizarre mistake that she'd been left behind. Her words seemed to transform into some other language before they reached people. They stood at the pumps, their faces puzzled, shaking their heads, saying "no, no," and Harper retreated quickly, so they could think they had imagined her, so they might wonder if it was all a strange joke.

She had a terrible headache, but didn't want to spend money on Tylenol in the little travel shop. When she refilled her Sprite for the third time, she wondered what time the rest stop closed, or when the food court closed down, but knew it would be an odd question to ask—nobody should be around long enough for such a thing to matter. Finally, she asked a dull-looking worker at the Kentucky Fried Chicken what time the food court closed.

"The food shuts down at eleven o'clock, but the rest stop and bathrooms stay open all night," he said.

She went back out to the scrubby field. Making sure no one was looking, she lifted a piece of flattened cardboard from the dumpster and dragged it back to the grass. She bent the cardboard and placed it against a scrawny tree, so she'd have something to sit on and lean against as she nursed Anna. Her arms were tired, and she looked down at the delicate cup of Anna's ear, brushed a mosquito away. Darkness fell on the flat world. The night was clear. It would have been pretty if she could feel a sense of peace.

A little after ten, Harper went back inside, staying out of the way of the food service employees. She hadn't eaten any dinner, afraid they'd recognize her from mid-afternoon. Harper slipped into the Ladies' Room and looked at herself in the mirror. She looked the same, which seemed extremely strange.

2

With Anna cuddled in the crook of her arm, Harper brushed her teeth, which was tricky to do one-handed: laying the toothbrush on the counter, undoing the tube of toothpaste with one hand, squeezing a little on, then getting the top back on. Brushing her teeth made her feel better. She went back to the scrubby field. There was no place to settle, and as hot as the day had been, she didn't want to sleep outside. It felt unprotected, and the mosquitoes didn't sleep.

Sitting down, she realized she should have changed into pants inside, but the idea of dragging Anna and her clothes back to the Ladies' Room was too much. She put Nate's Evergreen sweatshirt over her legs, her backpack behind her head, and laid Anna beside her. The sky was clear, stars pricking through, no moon. She thought about losing five hundred dollars and started to weep. Caleb would dump the car seat, never knowing the money was there. More than eight hundred dollars had seemed like a fortune; now she was down to a little more than three hundred. When she thought of changing Anna earlier, she felt a terrible regret. Anna hadn't been that wet, but Harper had changed her because she didn't want her to cry in the car. She had only twelve diapers left, and she had to get a ride before she ran out. There were no diapers for sale at the rest stop. If she ran out, no one would give them a ride; poop would be her final undoing. Harper squeezed her eyes shut. She wanted to scream, to sob, but it wouldn't help. Anna dozed on her chest.

In the middle of the night, Anna stirred, wakeful, and Harper took her inside to change her. Glancing at her watch, a little after 2 A.M., Harper felt seized by anxiety. There was so much more of the night to get through. She carried her things inside with her; everything was clean and quiet and empty. She wanted to lie down on the floor, put the changing mat and her sweatshirt down, but it would mark her as vagrant, and she couldn't risk it. Anna's diaper was a mess, and after she cleaned Anna up, changed her, Harper couldn't bear to go back outside.

Since no one was around, she left her backpack and diaper bag in the bathroom and, with Anna on her hip, dragged a chair into the bathroom and set it next to the changing table. She set Anna on the table, but the plastic seemed too hard. She pulled the changing mat out of her diaper bag, put it underneath Anna on the table, then put Nate's sweatshirt over her. That was better. She took the arms of the sweatshirt and tied them under the table; they barely reached, but Anna wouldn't fall off. Harper sat down in the chair and leaned against the table.

She didn't really sleep, but half-dozed through the night. Her butt kept falling asleep in the hard chair. Early the next morning, an old woman came in to use the bathroom, and Harper stood up, foggy-headed, and tried to pretend she was changing Anna. Her eyelids felt hot. Her stomach rumbled. When the woman left the Ladies' Room, Harper stretched her arms above her head. She leaned to one side, her body tingling in odd places. She leaned the other way, then brushed her hair and splashed water on her face. Drying it with a paper towel felt like sandpaper, but when she looked up, her face was smooth. No one, by looking at her, would have any idea of what had happened.

She decided to get some breakfast and have a cup of coffee, neither of which she usually did. She'd try for a ride again; maybe her luck would be better today.

After getting coffee and a muffin, Harper sat in the bright eating area. Anna rested in the crook of her arm, smiling her toothless smile, no idea of anything. At least there was that. To her, it was just another sunny day. As she drank her coffee, Harper tried to improve on her story from yesterday, but couldn't think of what to say that wouldn't sound strange. The fact was, if someone left you behind, wouldn't they come back? Or wouldn't your parents come get you?

She tried people at the pumps again, but had to be careful of anyone who might notice her or report her. Mid-morning, she changed a hugely messy diaper, and wiping Anna off, Harper felt a sense of panic. If she ran out of diapers, she was done. When they came out of the bathroom, with Anna in a dry diaper, Harper abandoned any pretense of trying to figure out who would be a good bet. She scanned for out of state plates—Illinois, Wisconsin, Minnesota—anyone who might carry her away. She tried a large Asian family with a mini-van and a bunch of little kids. The father, a short, wizened man, looked puzzled by her request. He had pumped the gas and was cleaning his windshield, and she thought he might say, 'Yes,' but he looked to his wife in the passenger seat and said something to her in an unfamiliar language. She looked at Harper and called to someone in the back of the van. A boy of about ten came forward and got out; his younger brothers and sisters poked their heads out the windows. Harper asked if she could have a ride, and he translated for his parents.

"Who left you here?" he asked.

"A family friend."

He relayed this to his parents, who said something back to him. "Where are your parents?"

"I don't have any," Harper said.

He translated, and the woman looked out at her. Harper could tell she didn't believe her.

She said something to the boy.

"I'm sorry, we have no room," the boy said.

He got back in the van and slid the door closed with a bang.

•

BY MID-AFTERNOON, THE sun was hot, Anna was

crying, and Harper felt dizzy with fatigue and gas fumes. She walked back towards the rest stop entrance, shifted Anna onto her other hip, and once inside the doors, sank down in a crouch and started to cry. She didn't want to be noticed, she was out of sight of the food court, but there was no place to really hide. She didn't want to go back to the stinky bathroom. It was disgusting to hide there. She put her head down against Anna and cried silently, chokingly. Then Anna started to cry, chiming in with her grief. Harper tried to take a deep breath. She slumped in the side of the doorway, one hand over her eyes, and sobbed.

"Young woman, are you all right?" A deep voice addressed her.

Harper looked up. A very tall, dark-skinned woman was looking down at her, and her tone implied that it was obvious that things weren't all right.

"My ride left me," she sobbed.

"What?"

"My ride. Someone was giving me a ride, and my baby cried, and he left."

"He just left you here? With a baby?"

Harper nodded, and started to weep again.

"Where are you going?"

Harper took a breath. If she said Olympia, Washington, the woman would bolt. She knew it. Where could she go? She thought of her father.

"To La Crosse, Wisconsin."

"Well, I'm going to Madison. I could take you that far."

"My brother goes to school there."

"Maybe he can get you to La Crosse."

Harper gulped. "I'd really appreciate it."

•

HARPER HAD NEVER had a conversation with a grownup black person before. "African American" was what you were supposed to say. That was what they learned in school. There were only three black kids in their high school; they hung together, and Harper didn't know their parents. She was afraid of saying the wrong thing to this woman, who said her name was Yvonne.

"Do you want to get yourself something to eat or drink? You look like you could use something."

Harper nodded, afraid she'd start to cry again.

"Let's put your things in the car. Then I can hold your little girl while you get some food."

They walked out to the parking lot. Yvonne had a blue Volvo station wagon, and they set the diaper bag and Harper's backpack in the back seat.

"You have money for food?" Yvonne asked.

"Yes," Harper said. "Can I get you something, too?" It seemed the polite thing to say.

Yvonne held up a soda. "I just ate. You get what you need."

Harper handed Anna to her. Yvonne smiled at Anna and shook her head to make her long earrings sway. "Go on now. Get what you need and let's get on the road."

Harper got a large juice, a cheese sandwich, and potato chips for later on. It felt strange to move, unencumbered, without Anna and the diaper bag. She carried her food back out to the car, where Yvonne cooed at Anna, who seemed transfixed.

"It's illegal for me to have the baby in a car without a carseat, but I suppose this is an unusual circumstance."

Harper nodded and waited for Yvonne to tell her what to do; she didn't want to disagree or give her a chance to change her mind.

"I think you should ride in back with the baby."

Harper climbed into the back seat, which she noticed was leather. Carefully, she set down her food and fastened her seatbelt. She reached for Anna.

"You're used to doing for yourself, aren't you?"

"Yes, I am."

Yvonne glanced down at the food at her feet.

"I'll be careful of your seats."

"There's a cupholder there. You can hold onto her and still reach what you want."

Harper said little in the next hour, simply tried to eat without spilling anything, while holding onto Anna. They drove down the highway in relative quiet. Anna fussed to be nursed, and then wasn't hungry when she did.

As they moved down the highway, Harper tried to feel relieved. She hadn't planned to stop in Madison. Once her mother realized Harper was missing, she'd probably call David, and Harper would have to beg him to let her stay, or move on without telling him where she was going.

"What do you do in Madison?" Harper asked.

"I'm an Economics professor at the University."

"I appreciate you giving me a ride."

"Well, you caught me on the way home from a conference. And I certainly don't know what else you'd do."

Harper thought of the families who had hurried around her, all the shoes walking by.

"Are you running away?" Yvonne asked.

"If you're eighteen, it's not running away, is it?"

"I suppose not. Why are you heading to La Crosse?"

"My father lives there."

"What does he do?"

"I don't know really. He and my mom aren't in touch."

Yvonne nodded and concentrated on the traffic ahead. Harper wished she could see her expression. Anna cried to be nursed again, and Harper shifted her to her other arm.

•

AS THEY CAME up on signs for Gary, Indiana, the smell

of sulfur seeped into the car. In the early summer evening, the sun was still high; miles of factories, variegated gray, spread around them. To the north, as far as Harper could see, were gargantuan buildings, columns of bilious smoke, an arsenal of gray pipes and fire. White fire flared up, chemical and unworldly. Hell on earth.

"Did they ever think it would get so big?"

"What would get so big?"

"Well, all this machinery, everything. I mean, a long time ago, when they used horses, it was probably blacksmith shops and railroads, but it spread into all this." Harper looked out at the gray landscape. "It's like Mordor."

"What's Mordor?"

"You know, from *The Lord of the Rings*, where all the bad guys are."

Yvonne smiled. "An industrial version. Did you read those books?"

"Well, I read *The Hobbit* over and over when I was a kid. I read the other books, too. They're long, but I didn't mind. They took up a lot of time."

"And that was good?"

"Yeah."

"Most people your age are in a hurry."

"Where I grew up, there was nothing to hurry to."

"What did you like about *The Hobbit*?"

The paperback copy she'd read over and over had soft, yellowed pages and a picture of the hobbit hill on the cover. "I liked the little houses in the hillside, the pantries underground and lots of little sweet meals." Harper smiled. "I kind of wanted to live on the Shire. I used to wish it was a real place I could go to."

Harper looked out at the lanes of traffic. She couldn't imagine driving here. The congestion, even as traffic was moving, made her feel hemmed in. They slowed in Chicago, where the tall metallic buildings gleamed, impenetrable, like Oz.

"Do you go to Chicago much?" Harper asked.

"I have colleagues who teach here, and I come in sometimes. I like to visit."

Anna's head, hot and sticky, rested in the crook of Harper's elbow. She shifted, so Anna's head would be leaning on her other arm. Yvonne gasped a little and slowed, leaving room in front of her. She was clearly nervous about having a baby in the car without a carseat. That first day, when Anna came home from the hospital, her mother never even thought about the precariousness of a new baby in a car. Harper looked around her—so many lanes! How could people stand to live here? They passed a mini-van on the side of the road with a frantic-looking woman leaning into the back.

As they got to the west side of the city, the traffic slowed. Harper wondered how much further it was to Madison. David was done with the school year now; he'd be working, doing landscaping again. She wasn't sure how he'd act when he saw her. She'd called him after Anna was born, but he'd asked the same question as her mother: "So, are you going to give her to those people?"

Yvonne glanced in the mirror, startled. "That baby is yours, isn't it?"

"Of course she is."

Her shoulders relaxed. "Foolish of me to think about that now. I had a moment of worrying I'd helped someone steal a baby."

"She's definitely mine. I'm nursing her."

"Of course, you're right, but you're not eighteen, are you?" Yvonne asked.

"I am."

"You know, I teach an undergraduate class now and then, so

I know what eighteen looks like." Yvonne sighed. "You stick to your story. It probably covers me in the long run."

"Have you lived in a lot of different places?" Harper asked.

Yvonne looked in the rearview mirror, surprised by the question. "Well, yes, I suppose. I lived in Philadelphia for a while, then Berkeley, then Missouri, and now Madison."

"Did you like one place best?"

"I liked Berkeley. I liked the city and the restaurants. I had a lot of friends there."

"I feel like I'm the only person I know who doesn't want to move to a city. I'd like to move to some cool little town where there's stuff to do, but not too much."

"Sounds like you're aiming for a college town."

"I guess I am."

They were both quiet for a while. Then the traffic started to flow more freely and sped out, beyond the reach of the city. Finally, Harper spotted a sign for Madison.

"So, what's your brother's address?" Yvonne asked.

Harper took a sweaty arm out from underneath Anna's legs and reached into her backpack. David had moved enough times during college that his newest address wasn't always clear in her mind. She pulled a piece of paper out of the front pocket of her pack and read Yvonne the address.

"I think I know where that is. Hilldale. Have you ever been to Madison before?"

Harper shook her head.

"It takes a few minutes to get there from the highway. Are you planning on college yourself?"

"I planned to—. I still want to go, but I'm not sure how I'm going to do it."

"Well, don't give up on the idea just because you have a child."

They pulled up in front of a large, white clapboard house

with four or five bikes locked on the front porch. The sky had grown purple; the house was dark. Yvonne got out, came around, and helped Harper get her things out of the car. She squinted up at the house.

"Your brother expecting you?"

"No, but it will be all right."

Yvonne studied her and Harper wished she could read her expression, which seemed stern, mask-like, as they stood in the diminished day.

"You seem pretty tough," Yvonne said. "Remember, not everything has to happen just when people say it has to. You can take care of your baby, but you should find a way to go to school. Get an education so you can do for yourself."

"Thank you so much," Harper said. "I'll never forget this."

Yvonne put her hand on Harper's shoulder. Her fingers were long, her nails a shade paler than her skin. She looked as if she might say something more. Then she turned and gave a brief wave before driving away.

16

HARPER PUT ON her backpack, slung her diaper bag over her shoulder, and held Anna against her. She walked up to the front door and rang the bell.

The door opened and a shirtless young man, beer in hand, peered out at her. "Well, trick or treat. What can I do you for, darling? Are you selling Girl Scout cookies?"

"Is David here?"

"David? The statue? Our man of marble? No, the god of landscaping will probably work until . . ." He squinted. "Well, until now. Sometimes, he goes out to have a few beers, some-times he comes home to shower first—depends on who he's trying to impress."

"I'm his sister. I'd like to come in and wait."

"Whoa! You're his kid sister? I'm sorry. Come on in."

She followed him into a sparsely furnished living room. A green couch, facing a large TV, sagged in the middle of the room. Bookshelves made of planks and glass blocks held stacks of books, a few dead plants, stacks of CDs. A White Sox poster was thumbtacked to the wall.

"David's room is probably a mess. Pig that he is. Have a seat—d'you want something to drink?"

"Sure." Shifting Anna from one arm to the other, she slid her backpack off.

He came back from the kitchen a minute later. "We have beer, and one lone Coke."

"Coke would be great." She didn't want to put Anna on the floor, the carpet looked ratty, but she wasn't sure what else to do. She took a baby blanket from the diaper bag, flicked it open on the carpet, then set Anna down. The boy flopped down in a recliner that seemed permanently set on flat.

"So, David told us that he was an uncle. This is your little girl?"

"Yes."

"Does your mom know you're here?"

Harper looked down at Anna, tried to think of what to say, when she heard the sound of keys in a lock, and David walked in the front door. He set down an empty water jug and a lunch box. He was deeply tanned, his T-shirt dirty, his jeans splattered with paint. He didn't recognize her in the gloom.

"Hey dude, what're you—"

"David!"

His expression registered surprise, then pleasure, then something else. He saw Anna on the floor. "What the—?"

Harper got up from the couch. She hadn't seen him since December and wondered if he'd be calmed by the fact that she was back to her normal size. He hugged her, smelling of sweat and salt and cedar chips and dirt, then looked over her shoulder at Anna. He followed Harper into the living room, where she picked Anna up.

"Do you want to hold her?"

David looked at Anna as if she were a strange object. "I'm all dirty. I'd be afraid to." He bent over, touching Anna's fingers, then looked at Harper. "What the hell are you doing here?"

Harper glanced at his roommate; she didn't want to tell the story in front of him. "Wait, let me get a beer," David said. "I just got off work."

He came back in, popped a beer, then flopped down on the sofa, facing her. He glanced over at his roommate, who stood up, seeming to get the hint.

"I'm heading out to Benny's—maybe I'll see you later on."

"Okay, later."

Harper waited until his roommate got out the front door before she spoke. "Mom wants me to get rid of Anna."

"Well, we know Mom's messed up, but in this case, she might be right."

Harper folded her arms and glared at him. She had never imagined they would be divided. She had always thought that, once she was out of the house, she and David could leave their mother behind

"I still don't get what you're doing here."

Harper wanted to tell David everything—about her dream, and escaping, about Caleb leaving her at the rest stop, but if she told him about the past few days, he'd be furious.

"Mom said she could have me declared unfit. She said she would make up a bunch of stuff, and Social Services would take Anna away."

"She was probably just drunk."

Harper looked down at Anna and suddenly felt older than David, as if they had inexplicably reversed positions. "Someone called from the county a few days ago, saying he heard I left Anna in a car."

"Did you?"

"Of course not! Mom made it up."

"How did you get here?"

She looked down at the floor and tugged on the edge of

Anna's blanket, straightening it. "I caught a ride."

"To Madison?"

"I thought," and her chin trembled, knowing already it wasn't going to work. "I thought I could stay here for a little bit. Just to get myself together."

"Harper! You can't stay here with a baby. If it was just me, it would be one thing, but I live with four other guys. It's their house, too. A college house isn't any place for a baby."

"I'm not planning to stay long. I've got $300."

"What would you do here? You can't work, because you'd have to pay someone to take care of the baby. What's your game plan?"

"I don't know. I just had to get out."

David got up and looked out the window in the dark. "You're looking for the baby's dad, aren't you?"

Harper folded her arms across her chest and looked down at Anna.

"Listen, let me save you some humiliation. Some guy who doesn't know he's a father is not going to be thrilled to see you. Is he from Madison?"

"I'm not going to find Anna's father. I'm going to La Crosse to talk to our dad."

David rubbed his hands over his face. "Please, don't do that."

"Why not?"

"It's not a good idea."

"How do you know?"

"I've seen him."

"You have! When?"

"I've seen him over the past few years."

"Why didn't you tell me?"

"You wouldn't like what you'd hear."

"What's wrong with him?"

"Nothing."

"What do you mean?"

David looked at her for a long moment, as if trying to decide what to say. He put his hands on his knees. "He's not your father."

Harper stared, thinking she hadn't understood. "What? Are you insane?"

"He's not your father. Do you really want to hear this?"

Anna started to fuss. Harper pulled her keys out of her pocket and dangled them in front of Anna. She kept her eyes on David.

David got up and flicked on the ceiling fan. The whirring blades caught Anna's attention.

"He found out, when you were little, that his best friend was really your dad—or at least that's what Mom told him. His best friend got killed in a car wreck, and he was busted up about the whole thing, and Mom told him that his friend was really your father, and he just couldn't take it."

Harper sat back on the couch and looked down at Anna gazing up at the fan. "So my father is actually dead?"

"Seems to be."

Harper felt her world rearranging itself, like a puzzle where the pieces don't quite fit. "That sucks," she said.

"Yeah, it does."

"How long have you been in touch with him?"

David leaned back, put his arms behind his head; his biceps bulged against his sleeves. "About two years. He'd send me birthday cards and stuff, like you, but at the end of my freshman year, I got drunk with some friends and went to see him, on a road trip, and we talked, and he told me why he left."

"How come you never told me?"

"What good would it have done?"

Harper stared at her apartment keys. Why had she saved

them? She set them on the dirty coffee table.

David drained his beer, set it on a side table, and looked at her. "Listen, I'm going to straighten up my room and change the sheets so you can sleep in my bed. I'm meeting some friends in a little while, and I have to think about all this. I work really early in the morning: I'm doing a job for some people who are having a big wedding in their backyard, so if the weather's good, I've got to go. But we've got to get you home. Mom must be worried. Have you called her?"

"Fuck no."

"Well, you should let her know where you are."

"She doesn't care."

"Of course she does."

Harper looked around the room. A white plastic clock sat on a small table in the corner. 9:43. She wouldn't tell him she'd been gone for one night already. Let him think she'd left this morning; it might buy her some time. "Jesus, David, there's no use in pretending. If she cared, wouldn't she have called here?"

"She probably didn't think you could get this far."

•

HOURS LATER, HALF-ASLEEP, Harper heard David come in to check on her. He bumped into something, cursed, went into the bathroom, back to the living room, and then it was quiet. Anna slept, her moist little fists curled by the side of her head. Harper squeezed her eyes tight against crying. She hadn't planned to come here, but when she did, she'd hoped to find relief. Clearly, this could only be a pitstop.

When Harper woke the next morning, her head felt heavy and groggy; the house was quiet. Anna was still asleep. Harper wanted orange juice or lemonade, then remembered David's roommate saying they only had beer. She sighed, wishing she lived in a place where people kept real food in the house. Sleep dust gummed the corners of Anna's eyes, and Harper gently touched the bits of gunk away. She had to find breakfast, had to stop thinking of herself as a child, or a person that someone else would provide for. If she wanted a house with food in it, she was going to have to figure it out for herself. Harper got up and tiptoed to the kitchen.

There was an envelope on the table with her name on it. She pulled out a note and a twenty dollar bill.

Harper. You need to call Mom today. There's a farmer's market down the street. Get yourself some food and we can talk tonight. You can't stay here long, but get what you need.

D.

Harper opened the refrigerator. Mountain Dew, Beer, Ketchup, Mustard, three old hamburger buns. A jar of relish. A pack of hot dogs. She heard Anna stirring and ran back to David's room.

Arranging a pillow against the wall, Harper sat up in bed, nursing Anna. She'd only been gone for two days, but it felt as if she'd been gone for weeks. Was there a Greyhound Station in Madison? She'd have to find a phone book and see. There was no train station; David had once said it was miles away, up by the interstate, and the train was always late. She'd have to find the Greyhound station, look for a convenience store or someplace she could get diapers along the way. Harper wished she could steal a car, leave it somewhere, steal another, but that was only in the movies. The police would pick you up, quick as anything, if you stole a car.

When she was done nursing Anna, Harper wanted a shower, but Anna might cry while Harper was in the bathroom, and she didn't know who else was in the house. What time was it? If there was only one bus a day, she'd better be on it.

She carried Anna into the living room and looked around for a phone book and a clock. The same roommate, wearing jeans and a T-shirt now, was sitting on the couch, the late morning sun streaming in.

"Wake and bake!" He lifted his beer in a gesture of cheers. "Your mother called. I let the machine pick it up." He gestured to a phone machine resting on a small table in the corner.

Harper's stomach trembled and she leaned Anna against her shoulder. Sunlight angling in the window lit the glaze of dust on the machine. She touched the button.

"David, it's Mom. Harper took off the other day for God knows where. She may have gone to talk to those folks about adoption, or gone off with those silly friends of hers. Anyway, if you hear from her, let me know."

The machine clicked to 0.

"Don't worry about it," Harper said. She wished the roommate would get out of the room so she could slip out unnoticed. "Do you have a phone book?"

He pointed to the graffiti on the wall above the phone. "That's it. We have a ritual scrubbing every semester."

Harper smiled wanly, then sniffed. Anna needed to be changed.

She went back to David's room to change her. Her mother's call was like a bell at the track, setting her in motion. She had to get out of here without the roommate knowing she'd really left.

She peeked in the top drawer of David's bureau, which was old and scratched, painted an ugly olive green. He must keep some cash here. She felt around under the jumble of boxer shorts, condoms, and socks, found a small tin box tucked in the back of his drawer, and opened it. Five twenties. He'd be pissed if she took it, but there wasn't time to ask. If she didn't say anything, David might think a roommate stole it. No, he'd guess it

was her. She looked down at Anna burbling on the bed. Harper
took the bills. She found a piece of scrap paper and a pen on
top of the dresser.

David,

I'm really sorry I had to take your money. I'll pay you back.
                                                    Harper

She repacked her backpack and the diaper bag, making
room for more diapers. She'd need wipes, too. She lifted Anna
into the Snugli, a soft weight at her chest, put on the backpack,
and pulled the diaper bag over her shoulder. Harper felt like a
pack mule, but she had to act like she was just going out for a
stroll. She crept out of David's room. In the living room, the
roommate was watching Saturday morning cartoons. She had
to pass him to go out the front door, so she walked through the
side of the room, trying to act casual.

"Tell David I'll see him later," Harper said.

"Later on," he said.

She stepped into the late June morning. A light breeze
blew across her shoulders. The world was open in front of her.
If she had more money, the feeling would be a relief. She started down the street, her stomach growling; she needed breakfast
and hoped the farmer's market was close.

The houses with their well-tended gardens were different,
more individual, than Mrs. Gallagher's house. The people on
the sidewalk looked well-nourished, intelligent, as if they had
interesting jobs or traveled to places they liked. They strolled
in couples or walked their dogs; everyone seemed to fit in here.
She kept her eyes open for a place that sold diapers, but there
weren't any stores. Her stomach tightened. Down a side street,
she spotted a red brick building. It was a drugstore, and she

found a pack of diapers, but they cost almost three dollars more than they would have at a big store. She wavered, considered stealing them, but the package was too bulky. She carried them to the counter.

Out on the step, she let the diaper bag off her shoulder, stuffed the diapers in, then lifted the bag to her left shoulder. A stroller would make things so much easier: she could have her stuff in a basket below Anna instead of carrying everything herself. She hoped the farmer's market was close.

She walked steadily, conserving her strength, murmuring to Anna. People coming toward her carried string bags of vegetables, sacks of bread and baked goods. When they pointed their key fobs at their expensive cars, the cars unlocked, lights blinked, like sleek mechanical pets. A few blocks from the market, she realized she should have asked about the Greyhound station or looked at a phone book in the drugstore, but it was too far to go back. *I just need to get something to eat*, she told Anna. *We'll find the station and get a ticket there.*

At the farmer's market she bought juice and two strawberry-rhubarb muffins from the first stand she found. Harper carried them off to the side, lay Anna down on her back, and ate quickly. The sour taste of rhubarb against the cakey sweetness was wondrous.

She sat crosslegged in the grass, watching the crowd of shoppers, reluctant to pick up her burdens again. Finally, wanting something else to eat, she got up to wander the lines of stalls, looking at jams and fruits, candles and soap, all kinds of vegetables. She stopped in front of one table because she liked its banner: a circle of hearts, HARMONY VALLEY FARM.

Old friends were greeting one another, or someone had come back from somewhere, because there was lots of exclaiming and *how-are-you's*? A man with deep-set eyes, tired and sunburned, sat off to the side. She looked over the array of vegetables and melons, touched a green leafy vegetable with a bright red stalk.

"What's this?" Harper asked.

"It's chard," he replied. "Never had it?"

"No." She started to say her mother didn't like to cook, but stopped herself. It didn't matter anymore.

"It's great steamed with beet tops."

"I didn't know beets had tops."

A curly-haired boy of seven or eight looked at her and grinned, as if she'd made a joke.

"I'm Leonard. This is my son Ryan—he grows these melons." Leonard extended his hand, which looked as if dirt was permanently etched into the cracks. When Harper shook his hand, she felt callouses on his fingers.

Pale, golden melons glistened in the middle of the table. "They're beautiful," she said to the boy.

"Here." Leonard took a melon set on ice, cut into it, and handed her a slice. "Tell me that isn't the best thing you've ever had."

The melon was sweet and cold and unbelievably good. She nodded, wished she could give some to Anna.

"I like your sign." She glanced up at the banner. "You don't need anyone to work for you, do you?"

Leonard studied her. "Mostly, we hire in early spring for summer. It's hard to imagine how you'd work and take care of a baby."

"I know." Harper flushed, and walked along the stall, surveying the other vegetables. Lots of things she'd never even heard of. Three different kinds of lettuce. She'd never seen lettuce so green.

"You don't grow the regular kind?"

"What do you mean 'the regular kind?'" A woman at the other end of the stall looked at her.

"You know, what you buy in the store."

"Iceberg lettuce? It's round, pale green?"

Harper nodded.

"No, we don't grow that. It doesn't have much nutritional value. These taste much better." She touched a small head, with loose, red-tinged leaves. "This buttercrunch is really sweet."

Harper didn't see how lettuce could be sweet. She guessed the woman was being kind to her, that it would be easy to make fun of her for asking about iceberg lettuce.

She moved down the row, thinking she should buy food that she could take on the bus, something that wasn't heavy. She stopped at a stall where a man was selling Amish jams and jellies, coffee mugs and scones. The mugs—earth-colored splashed with blue, or cranberry swirled with pale white—were beautiful. She picked up a mug; it felt nice in her hand.

The man sat in a chair, watching her, then said, "If there's anything you want, let me know."

His reddish thinning hair—a long forehead as Janet would say—gave him an anxious, outgrown look. Red hairs ran from his chin down his neck. His clothes looked as if they came from a flea market. She picked up a saucer-sized dish, wondering what it was for.

Rising stiffly out of the chair, he turned, and started lifting boxes from under his table. An old pickup was parked behind his stall.

"I didn't know Amish drove cars."

"I'm not Amish."

She looked down at the jam: gooseberry, boysenberry, flavors she'd never heard of.

There wasn't much left on the table.

"I live out in the country, near a couple Amish farms, so I sell some for the Amish, which gets me the stall. The ceramics are mine."

"Where do you live?"

"Out near Viroqua."

"Where's that?"

"Vernon County, 'bout forty miles from La Crosse."

"My father lives in La Crosse. I'm going to see him. I haven't seen him in a couple years." Harper picked up a jar and turned it in front of Anna, as if showing her a faceted jewel. "My boyfriend was giving me a ride, and we had a fight, and he left me."

"Your boyfriend is an asshole."

Harper grinned. "Do you know if there's a Greyhound bus station around here?"

His eyes narrowed. "In Mad-town? Not likely. Wouldn't your father come get you?"

She set the jam down. "I'm not sure he'd come this far."

"Then your dad's an asshole, too."

She looked down at the dust-covered grass, worn by setting up and breaking down. She was so tired of carrying all this stuff. What could she do if there wasn't a bus station here?

Harper lifted her gaze to his truck.

"Would you give me a ride?"

"I'm not going to La Crosse."

"Just to that town you said."

He looked at Anna. "With the baby?"

She nodded.

"If the baby cries, you're both sitting in back."

"Deal," Harper said.

17

THE PICKUP WAS a copper-colored Nissan, the wheel wells so rusted that the truck appeared to be two colors. From the way he loaded the boxes into the back, three at a time, she guessed they were mostly empty.

"Do you usually leave early?" Harper asked.

"Morning's the busy time here. Most of my business is done by noon. No point in hanging around."

"What's your name?" Harper asked.

"Dorn."

"Door?"

"Dorn—like corn."

Harper couldn't help but smile. "How'd you get a name like that?"

"Long story," he said.

She lay Anna down in the grass and changed her while he finished packing up. The diaper bag was bulging now and heavy. It didn't matter, she thought. She'd be riding, not walking. After he loaded the boxes, she put her diaper bag and backpack in back, wedging them between the boxes and the tailgate so there was no chance they could fly out. Her money was in the front pocket of her shorts.

She climbed into the front seat with Anna. The sides of the truck felt thin; she hoped he was a good driver. As he navigated the small streets outside the farmer's market, a car pulled up on a side street, and Dorn held up his left hand, as if to say, "Don't you dare pull out." A few blocks later, Dorn honked and cursed at a car in front of him. "Drivers in Madison are the worst," he said. A nervous grinding tightened her stomach, as if she were on the slow part of a roller coaster, rattling upward before the downward rush. Taking a deep breath, she let it out slowly.

Outside of Madison, the countryside was green with gentle hills, and Harper hoped that driving in a less populated area would aggravate him less. The hills gave the landscape a kind of privacy, a sense there were hidden houses and valleys just out of sight.

"Still a fair number of family farms in this part of Wisconsin," Dorn offered. "Out towards Vernon County there's a pretty large alternative community—lots of people living off the grid."

"Off the grid?"

"They don't buy electricity from the power company. They use solar, wind, heat with wood, all that."

Harper had never heard of such a thing. What did they do for air conditioning? She rolled her window down further. The afternoon was warm, and Anna seemed hot. At the farmer's market, Anna had been awake, looking around, but now she slept in Harper's lap.

"Is there a motel in Viroqua?"

"I suppose. There's some Bed & Breakfast places, for tourists. People come to canoe on the Kickapoo River."

Maybe one of the B&Bs needed a housekeeper. Mrs. Wood would give her a good reference. Harper chewed the inside of her cheek. If someone called the Motel 6 to check a reference, Social Services might find her. Or maybe they didn't bother if you left the state. In a few weeks it might not matter; after her eighteenth birthday, they couldn't make her go back.

She wondered if her mother would insist on her story, if her claim that Harper was unfit could follow her. Her mother wasn't the type to take things back. Still, Mrs. Wood would stick up for her. Her first impression of Mrs. Wood—a middle-aged woman in a suit—had changed: her long face had become comforting and familiar. Mrs. Wood would wonder what had happened to her, and Janet wouldn't think to explain why Harper had left.

"I really appreciate you giving me a ride," she said.

"Don't mind helping someone in a tight spot."

They drove for a while without talking. Dorn glanced over at her when she nursed Anna, but mostly kept his eyes on the road. She was glad he had to drive, and she looked out the window and studied the landscape. Two days ago, she would have freaked out about riding in the front of a ratty pickp truck without a car seat, but now, as they drove through countryside, Harper started to relax. It would be hours before David was home. Even if he went to the farmer's market and asked around, everyone would have left. There'd be no way to find her.

She'd try the B&B when they reached Viroqua; hopefully, it wouldn't be too expensive. What would she do from there? Should she call her father? Even if he wasn't her father, it was hard to stop thinking of him that way. David or her mother might contact him, so going to La Crosse seemed risky. Still, he might lie for her, let her stay a few weeks. She wondered if her father really was dead, or if there was any chance that the man she'd thought of as her father could be the real one. Maybe her mother had said what she did to hurt him. It was the kind of thing she'd do. If there was no chance at all that he was her father, why would he have bothered with things like birthday cards? If they met face to face, would she know for sure?

"How big is Viroqua? Does it have stores?"

"Some. A food co-op. Little bookstore. Real Estate offices. Coffee shop. Walmart, the evil empire. That kind of thing."

Up ahead, a horse and buggy trotted by the side of the road, an orange triangle on the back of the carriage. The horse's front feet winged out to the sides. As they passed, Harper leaned over to catch a glimpse of who was inside the carriage: a man and two children. Dorn waved, and the farmer waved back.

"The Amish have farms around here?"

"Sure do. They own their own places, too, do it all without banks." Dorn's voice was approving.

Harper bent over to kiss the top of Anna's head and noticed the "Check Engine" light was on. Fear moved in her. Dorn hadn't seen it yet. Were they close to town? She couldn't bear one more mishap. At the bottom of a hill, Dorn put his foot on the gas, but the truck slowed. He looked down at the dashboard.

"Mother fucking son of a bitch!"

Steam rose from the hood, and he swerved to the side of the road, the truck skidding in the gravel.

"Get out of the truck!" he yelled.

Harper held Anna tight and hopped out. She ran to the back and reached over the tailgate, banging the inside of her arm, the pain radiating out with a strange throbbing. She grabbed her backpack, tossing it off to the grass, then grabbed the diaper bag, yanking it up and tossing it to the side of the road. Anna was so sleepy that it was hard to keep her upright. Harper stepped away from the truck and moved the diaper bag and her backpack farther back, to a grassy spot near the edge of a cornfield, then stood in the grass with Anna while Dorn popped open the hood. Smoke billowed from the engine. He stepped back, cursing.

Harper closed her eyes against the sun. "How far are we from town?" she called.

"Huh?"

"How far is town?"

"A couple miles, two or three maybe."

Anna started to fuss, and Harper shifted her weight from foot to foot, rocking her back and forth. Dorn would probably be here for a while, and she guessed he wouldn't be pleasant. Two miles wasn't that far to walk, but with Anna, her backpack, and the damn diaper bag, it would take a while. She sat down to nurse Anna before setting out. Dorn clenched his fists and cursed, kicked the gravel as he waited for the engine to cool. With his scraggly beard and loose-jointed limbs, he looked like a pissed-off cartoon character. He was too old to be pitching such a fit. From the comments he'd made about not using banks, living off the grid, she doubted he had a cell phone to call for a tow.

After Anna finished nursing, Harper pulled the Snugli out of her diaper bag, put it on herself, and got Anna into it. Dorn leaned under the hood, checking the engine.

"I think my radiator cracked."

"You'd need a ton of water to get it to town," Harper said.

She put the backpack on, then slung the diaper bag over her shoulder. God, what a pain all this crap was. Anna snuggled against her.

"Is this the road into town?" Harper nodded up the hill.

"It sure is."

"I've got to get going."

"Thanks for nothing," Dorn said. He slapped his palms against his thighs.

She looked at him puzzled. "Did you want me to wait with you?"

"Guess not." He turned away.

Clearly he had hoped for more from her, but she couldn't think about it now. "Bye then," she said, and headed up the road.

She started up the hill, humming a little to Anna to keep a rhythm, but by the middle she could only breathe and put one foot in front of another. Parched, breathless, sweat-soaked, she didn't want to stop while he might be watching. After about twenty minutes, when she reached the top, there was no sign of a town. Would he be cruel enough to point her in the wrong direction? Looking down at Anna, Harper realized she should be wearing a hat. She stopped, pulled the diaper bag off her shoulder, put Anna's hat on, and then slung the bag over her other shoulder. As she started walking again, it bumped against her hip. She passed a geodesic house, covered in reddish wood. Cars whizzed by. The late sun beat down, and she whispered to Anna, hoping they were heading in the right direction.

Okay, here we go now. We'll find a place to stay tonight and then we'll think about what to do. My father isn't my father. Isn't that weird? All this time I thought he was. I told Dorn I was going to La Crosse. We might still go there. I don't know. I could ask him about my real father, but he might be angry. I could pretend I don't know that he's not my real dad, since he's been pretending all this time. Maybe he'd give us some money. He must know what a bitch Mom is. He did leave after all. The diaper bag thumped against her hip, rubbing it; she couldn't relax her arm by her side. A few days ago, with more than eight hundred dollars, it had seemed possible to get to Olympia, Washington, to run into Nate, to make some kind of start for herself. Now, nothing seemed likely. She felt as if she'd been gone a week, but it had only been a few days. She'd had so many unexpected conversations in the past few months—the Anderssons, the gym teacher, Katie's mother, Mrs. Wood. It was hard to tell who would turn out to be nice, and who would be mean. She liked the people at the farmer's market, the way Leonard had explained to her about chard, the way he'd gently put his hand on his son's head, the way the boy was growing things, too.

After an hour, she came to the outskirts of Viroqua, which didn't look like a tourist town. It seemed more country than Milan. She passed a real estate office, a hospital, a gem store with a huge geode in the window, an outfitters' place with canoes. Anna was sleeping again. Harper glanced at the side streets, looking for a B&B. Sweat ran down her back, under her breasts. A shower would feel so good.

She passed two women on the street, both with narrow faces and large overbites—one middle-aged, one very old—they must be mother and daughter.

"Excuse me, is there a B&B near here?"

"There's one two blocks up," the woman said. "On Maple Street. It's just a block or so in."

Harper smiled and thanked her. Up ahead, on a shady side street, she spotted a large Victorian house with a sign out front. She walked down a sidewalk cracked by tree roots and stopped in front of an elaborately painted house. There was no one around to bother her diaper bag, so Harper left it on the side of the path, one less thing to carry, as she climbed the front steps. She rang the doorbell.

A gray-haired woman came to the door, but didn't open the screen. Harper asked about rooms.

"I'm sorry. We don't have any vacancies."

Harper felt a chill. "Is there another B&B in town?"

"There's one out on Main Street, a few blocks from here."

Harper turned, trying not to let the woman see her distress. A few blocks seemed like forever. At the end of the path she picked up the diaper bag, and walked the way the woman indicated. She lifted Anna's hat and touched her lips to Anna's head. Her scalp seemed hot; Harper felt a ripple of fear. What if Anna was sick? Her head was down; she seemed to be dozing, and Harper didn't want to wake her up to check her. She put her hat back on. It was hard to tell anything since Harper was so hot herself. Could Anna have gotten too much sun while they were walking up the hill? Harper walked in the direction the woman had indicated. She didn't see the B&B. Perhaps she'd gone too far. Maybe it was on the other side? She couldn't keep wandering around with her pack, Anna, the diaper bag rubbing, through her shorts, to a raw place on her hip. As she hiked the bag up onto her shoulder for what seemed like the millionth time, Harper stumbled on something in the sidewalk. She felt herself falling, could almost see herself, as if in slow motion. She put her hands in front of the Snugli, over Anna's head, and tried to take a step forward, to catch herself, but the diaper bag swung forward and both of her knees hit the cement hard, her right knee grinding down first. It had been years since she'd skinned her knees, but God, it hurt, the burn and sharp fall: no cushion between skin and bone. Blood pounded in her chest and arms. It hurt too much to yell. She was still for a moment, caught in kneeling posture. Harper reached for the stone fence by the sidewalk, got herself upright, and looked down at her knees, both skinned and bleeding, sand and gravel stuck to the blood. If Anna wasn't sleeping next to her chest, she'd scream. Tears filled her eyes.

Grief stuck in her throat. She shook out her legs, her right knee was bleeding a lot, God it hurt. She wanted to weep, but couldn't just stand there on the sidewalk, crying. What could she clean herself with? Diaper wipes would work, but they'd sting. She had to find a place where she could set Anna down. Harper looked up to see two women on a deep front porch with a sign above them. The other B&B. A woman in a flowered dress hurried down the steps toward her. They must have seen her fall. The other woman, who Harper guessed was a visitor by the way she seemed in motion, on her way to someplace else, disappeared into the house. The flowered woman picked up her diaper bag, took Harper's arm and led her up to the porch.

"You took quite a fall there, let me help you."

Harper wanted to cry; she tried to take a deep breath. "I was just coming here, actually. Do you have any vacancies?" The torn skin on her knees hurt as she climbed the steps. Blood from her right knee ran down into her sock. She had to stop it; she didn't want her socks to get stained. She only had three pairs.

"Yes, we do." The woman gestured that Harper should sit down on the porch swing. "Is your baby okay?"

Harper looked down at Anna who'd been startled awake, her cheeks a flushed red. "I think so. I just wanted to make sure she didn't fall."

"Your knees took the brunt of it. Zoe went inside to get something to clean you up."

"What's your rate for a room?"

"One hundred forty dollars a night."

Harper's eyes filled up. "You don't have anything less expensive?"

"I'm sorry, I don't."

Harper reached around to loosen the straps of the Snugli, which was hard to sit down in. She concentrated on the straps. It was too much money, just too much. What was she going to do? She wished for a shower; she felt hot and disgusting. The other woman, Zoe, came back onto the porch.

"Why don't you let me clean up your knees?" Zoe had paper towels, a damp washcloth, and a bottle of peroxide. A large towel was flung over her shoulder.

Harper swallowed.

"We can set your baby down here." Zoe doubled the towel for cushioning and laid it on the porch in the shade.

They helped Harper lay Anna down, but Anna started to fuss. Harper leaned over and put her hand on Anna's head. Her forehead seemed hot and dry.

Zoe knelt in front of her, trying to gently wash off the sand and blood, and Harper remembered a commercial from when she was a kid. The commercial was for Bactine, which claimed not to hurt. Her own mother had never done anything like this; she'd never done anything tenderly. Harper began to sob.

"Are you all right, my dear?" The woman in the flowered dress hovered over her, patting the air above Harper's shoulder.

"Ginny, maybe a cold drink would be good. If you had some juice cut with water for her, or lemonade. Do you have a thermometer?"

Ginny nodded and went into the house.

"I haven't hurt your knee, have I? It's something else, isn't it?"

Harper looked at the woman crouching in front of her and nodded through her tears. The woman's face was tan and square, softly lined, her dark brown hair was short, but soft, tinged with gray. She had hazel eyes, green and brown, the color of moss and logs.

"Are you on your own?"

Harper nodded. "I'm afraid my little girl is too hot. If she has a fever, I don't know what to do."

The woman came back with a tall glass of lemonade for Harper.

"Ginny, do you have a thermometer, one that we can put under the baby's arm?"

"Oh, I forgot! Let me look." And she went back into the house, the screen door slapping behind her.

Anna started to cry, a high, thin sound.

"Why don't you drink something, then nurse her? We'll finish your knees in a few minutes." Zoe reached down and picked up Anna, smiled at her, then placed her in Harper's arms.

Harper drained the lemonade in a few gulps, then nursed Anna as they swayed back and forth in the swing.

"We'll see if Ginny has a thermometer. I bet your little girl is fine. Her color's good.

You may both be a bit dehydrated. Have you had much to eat today?"

Harper tried to think: muffins at the market, some melon, some raspberries. "Not a lot," she said.

"You need to eat and drink a lot when you're nursing a baby."

Harper nodded. "I know. Everything's been kind of hectic, though." Hectic was a ridiculous way to describe the last few days. She felt strange, light-headed. "Do you have kids?"

"I have a daughter who's grown. But I do EMT work, so I know a little."

"What's EMT?"

"Emergency Medical Technician. I ride in an ambulance when they ask me to, but I live out in the country. Sometimes I give the Amish a ride to the hospital."

"They go to hospitals?"

"Yes, but they can't drive themselves."

"Oh," Harper said.

Ginny came back with a thermometer, and Zoe put it under Anna's arm. "Ginny, would you mind getting her some more lemonade?"

Anna looked better in the shade, but she still seemed limp. The thermometer beeped. "A little over 100 degrees," Zoe said.

Fear knotted Harper's stomach. If Anna got sick it would be her fault. She'd be found unfit. Harper put her face in her hands and started to sob.

"Sh, sh, it's okay," Zoe said. "Babies get fevers like this all the time. The fever burns out whatever little bug they have. If it's a problem, you can go over to the clinic, but these things are usually gone overnight."

"I don't have anywhere to go," Harper cried.

"How did you get here?"

"I got a ride from Madison."

"Is that where you're from?"

Harper shook her head, tears running down into her mouth. Zoe went back to work on Harper's knees, talking as she worked.

"Listen, why don't you come home with me for the night? I live just a little south of town. I've got a spare room—two, in fact—and my husband won't mind."

Harper looked down at the woman's face. What else could she do? She nodded.

After getting Harper cleaned up, and taking Anna's temperature again, Zoe said a few words to her friend, then put Harper's bags in the trunk of her car. She held Anna while Harper got in and fastened her seatbelt, then passed Anna back to her.

"We haven't really been introduced. My name is Zoe," she said.

18

THAT NIGHT, AFTER Harper had showered and eaten,
after Zoe's husband had gone to bed, while Anna slept, Harper
told Zoe everything. She told her about Nate, and the rubber breaking, and about not being able to go through with an
abortion. She told about how loyal Janet and Katie had been.
She told about her mother and the karaoke night, how her
mother wanted her to give Anna up, how her mother had lied
to Social Services. Zoe asked only a few questions, mostly to
clarify who Harper was talking about at different parts in her
story. When Harper was done talking, she sat back, as if deflat-
ed.

Zoe put a hand on her shoulder. "All the things you told
me, let's just say you left out the part about not being eighteen
yet."

"You won't tell on me, will you?"

Zoe looked down at her hands. Her little fingers were
curved in a way that Harper had never seen before.

"No, I won't. I was a social worker for a while, and I saw

things I wish I hadn't. My guess is that you did the right thing to get out. I'll talk to Rick about letting you stay with us for a bit. Just to get your legs under you. He won't mind. He's a good man. The best I know, really."

Harper nodded, grateful. Zoe's husband had said very little and then gone to bed early. Harper couldn't read him. Zoe seemed trustworthy. She hoped so. She didn't know what else to do.

That night, when Harper went into the bathroom to brush her teeth, she found a bottle on the edge of the wide porcelain sink. Dr. Bronner's Magic Soaps. The label was covered with tiny writing. *Absolute cleanliness is next to Godliness! Who else but God gave man Love that can spark mere dust to life! Poetry, uniting All-One! All brave! All life! Who else but God! The whole World is our country, our Fatherland, because all mankind are born its citizens! We're all Brothers and Sisters because One, ever-loving Eternal Father is our only God, our only Religion, that Reunites God's legion! For we're ALL-ONE OR NONE. "LISTEN CHILDREN ETERNAL FATHER ETERNAL ONE!"* It went on and on like that, hundreds of words squeezed onto the label. Was it a joke? Did the people who made the soap really believe it? She squeezed some into her palm and the smell of peppermint overwhelmed her. It smelled like Nate.

•

THE NEXT MORNING, it took Harper a moment to remember where she was. She'd been dreaming about the rest stop with its sleek plastic surfaces; she was like Alice in Wonderland, falling down a white plastic rabbit hole with nothing to hang onto. She stretched in bed, trying not to wake Anna. It felt so good to be clean and to wake in a nice place. The silence was enormous. No cars, no wind, no music. A rapid knocking, too precise for human sound, hammered in the distance. Anna stirred, eyes moving behind her delicate eyelids.

Dust lined the soft crease in her neck; she needed a bath. Her forehead was cool to the touch.

Last night, it had been deep dusk by the time they arrived, so it was hard to see where they had landed. She wanted to get up, but Anna started to fuss, so Harper nursed her in the small sunny room. The elongated windows made bright rectangles of light on the wood floor; the wavy glass was like the windows in the Edison house. Outside, birds chattered, wind moved through the trees, a cow mooed in the distance. When she got up to dress, Harper saw that her room looked out the front of the house, over a gravel road to a field. Zoe had said there was a stream, but from her window, Harper saw only a line of trees in the distance.

Anna's diaper was heavy, and Harper changed her, put on a clean shirt, brushed her hair, and carried Anna down to the kitchen. Zoe perched on a stool, looking out the window, a large ceramic mug in her hands. In the morning sun, the deep lines of her face seemed sorrowful. Then she turned toward Harper and smiled, the wrinkles softening along her cheekbones. A coffee cake, half-eaten, sat on the table.

"Good morning," Harper said.

"Morning. Do you want some tea?" Zoe asked. "Coffee cake?"

"Thanks, that would be great." Harper felt slightly formal, afraid she'd said too much last night; she didn't want Zoe to change her mind about letting her stay. "Did you make this cake?"

"Yes, this morning."

"Did I sleep that late?" Harper looked around for a clock.

"No, I just get up early to make Rick lunch and see him off." Zoe stepped down off her stool. "I'll hold Anna while you eat something. Let me put some water on. Come see what sort of tea you'd like."

Zoe put a kettle on a large stove with six burners. Dried herbs, tied in neat bunches, hung from a thick beam in the ceiling. One wall, its counter lined with glass canisters, was dominated by a large, stainless steel refrigerator. Why did they have such large appliances when they didn't have kids to feed? The kitchen seemed the most modern room in the house.

"This morning I heard this fast knocking sound outside. I couldn't figure out what it was," Harper said.

"Oh, it's that woodpecker! Last year, he started drilling on the house, near our bedroom. I wanted to shoot him." Zoe pointed to boxes of tea on the counter. "Choose what you'd like."

The brightly colored boxes looked like a stack of small gifts; she picked them up, one by one. "I didn't know you could really hear woodpeckers like that."

"Unfortunately, you can."

Herb tea, black tea. Some of the boxes had little pictures and sayings on them. She held one up—with little bears on it—for Anna to see. Was choosing the right tea like choosing a wine? Was there a right thing to choose with coffee cake? In the morning?

"Here," Zoe said. "Try this." She handed Harper a yellow box that said Lemon Zinger, and Harper, relieved to have the decision made for her, dropped a teabag into a mug.

Zoe carried a jar of honey and a plate for coffeecake to the table. Harper felt almost embarrassed at the way Zoe tended to her. Why couldn't her own mother have done such a thing?

"Want me to hold her while you eat?" Zoe reached for Anna, who settled into her arms.

"Where does Rick work?"

"Well, we do some farming here, but he does computer work over at Organic Valley."

"What's that?"

"It's a company in La Farge. They sell milk, orange juice, mostly dairy products. They've just built a big new facility."

"Are you sure he doesn't mind I'm here?" Last night, lying in bed, Harper wondered if Rick had gone to bed early because he was mad that Zoe brought her home.

"I told him I'd like to let you stay a bit, to get yourself together. He doesn't mind."

"He's not mad about Anna?"

Zoe picked up her mug and sipped, steam rising around her face. "What's to be mad about?"

"Well, you know, babies cry, all that."

Zoe laughed. "My goodness. Such a small thing. It's nice to have a baby in the house." She smoothed her hand over a purple cloth napkin shot through with blue and green. "I have a daughter from my first marriage, but she's done with college, out and about in the world, and nowhere near having a baby, so this is fun for me. Rick doesn't have any children, but he likes to have them around."

"Most people wouldn't take in a stranger."

"Well, people do all kinds of things. Besides, the garden is full. We have more food than we can eat."

"Do you have a job in town?"

"I work for the school district, tutoring students in reading, but only during the school year. In summer, the garden keeps me pretty busy. We grow a fair amount of food, and I can it, or freeze it. We have other projects, too."

"Like what?" Harper sipped her tea.

"Well, we keep bees in a corner of the property, and we collect honey in the fall, but that's mostly for us or for gifts. Rick raises chickens, so there are the chickens to tend to and eggs to collect. He has meat chickens, too, and we slaughter some of them in the fall. There's a lot to do, in every season really."

The coffee cake was delicious. It had an unfamiliar spice,

rich and fragrant. She chewed carefully and waited until her mouth was empty before speaking.

"I don't know about the bees, but I'll try to help with the other stuff, if I can. This cake is really good." Harper felt as if she could eat and eat. She spooned honey into her tea, then licked the spoon, the sweetness thick in her mouth.

•

THAT FIRST DAY, Harper tended to Anna, gave her a bath, and tried to help Zoe around the garden and the house. Trailing after her felt awkward, but Zoe seemed to like the company. She took little breaks from gardening and watched Harper with Anna.

"She's a beautiful baby," Zoe said.

Harper felt a quiet pride. "I know, and she seems pretty happy, too. I mean, she cries, but it's mainly when she's hungry. My mother kept saying that she'd be fussy, that it would drive me crazy. But the truth is, she's all I've had to do. I mean, it is hard to take care of a baby, sometimes. But she's good."

"Well, it's probably because you're with her, and you talk to her, and keep her around. I brought my daughter everywhere with me, and she was happy, too, and as she got older, I think that early time together made her more secure. When she started school, she didn't blink about getting on the bus, or fuss about leaving—she was ready." Zoe lifted her hand, as if to wave, then seemed chagrined by her own half-gesture. She dropped her hand into her lap.

Zoe spent most of the day working in the garden. Beans needed to be staked. Tomatoes needed wire baskets to support them as they grew. Potatoes needed earth fluffed up at the base of the plants. Zoe made mounds of earth in a place where she'd already harvested something and let Harper plant squash. Five seeds, a knuckle deep, in the top of each mound. Zoe explained that she timed her plantings so that not everything was ready at once.

"I knew this existed, but I didn't know what it was like," Harper said.

"You mean having a garden? Lots of people do this."

They sat on the lawn and watched Anna waving her arms in a shady spot on the grass.

"In Milan, I always felt like I was in the wrong place, but I didn't know what the right place was." Harper leaned back, placed her palms on the ground, and looked up towards the line of trees in the distance. "I feel like other people have some idea of what their life should look like, but I don't have any idea at all. And now that I have Anna, there's a whole other person I have to take into account."

"Believe me, there are loads of people who feel that way. People a lot older than you. Especially when something big happens—like a divorce, or losing a job. You still have time to go to college, figure things out; it just might not be on the timetable you imagined."

"Look, oh, look!" Harper said. "Anna's rolling over!" And sure enough, she did.

•

AS THE DAYS passed, Harper felt an odd mixture of restlessness and relief. She wondered if anyone was looking for her and hoped they were not. She remembered Matt walking away, his expression of disgust. The fruit doesn't fall far the from the tree. Was it possible to simply step away from your past? She wanted to call Katie and Janet, hear their voices, find out if her mother was looking for her, but Zoe's number would appear on their cell phones, and Harper hadn't come this far to be dragged back.

•

RICK RETURNED FROM work one evening and, leaving a bag of groceries in the kitchen, went directly upstairs. He was often gone by the time she got up in the morning, and it was hard to tell if his quiet was due to shyness, a bad mood, or if it was just his nature. He did chores after work and listened to Zoe and Harper talk over dinner, sometimes interjecting a teasing comment, but mostly he was silent. In the evenings, reading, he touched the side of his beard near his ear. Rising from a chair, he moved slowly, as if his back hurt. That evening, Harper heard him moving around upstairs. She'd left some dirty clothes in a pile on the floor. Was he dissatisfied with how she kept her room? He came downstairs and said:

"There's a little something upstairs."

Harper's heart thudded. She hadn't left a soiled diaper upstairs, had she? Harper and Zoe went up, Rick following. Next to Harper's bed was a large bassinet with tiny blue and white flowers, lace edging the top.

"I know that blue isn't necessarily for girls, but it was the only color they had, and I thought it was pretty."

Harper stood still, stunned. Rick looked embarrassed. She took a step forward and hugged him; she only came up to his chest. She murmured into his shirt, which smelled of hay and chicken feed. "Thank you so much."

He patted her hair, as if unsure it was all right to touch her. "It's nothing," he said. "Nothing at all."

•

AT NIGHT, WHEN she tried to sleep, the question of her future swirled around her. She didn't want to overstay her welcome, but helping around the house was the only thing she could think of to do. Zoe seemed to like having them, but Zoe treated her the way you'd treat someone fragile, and Harper was afraid she'd tire of this. Thinking of the bassinet, Harper smiled in the dark.

She could imagine Rick in a store, in coveralls and thick shoes, studying the baby things. She thought of Nate. Should she get in touch with him? Maybe Zoe would know a way.

•

ONE AFTERNOON, HARPER and Zoe sat on the lawn, eating cheese sandwiches and cucumber salad. Anna grabbed at the grass, and when she tried to put it in her mouth, Harper pulled the few blades from her moist fist.

"You know, when Anna was brand-new, I wished there was another person around, just to talk to, or hold her sometimes. You've been really great."

"Well, we like having you, and it's nice to have a baby in the house. My first husband . . . well, he had a vasectomy while I was in the hospital having my daughter," Zoe said.

Harper was quiet for a moment, thinking she must have misunderstood. "That's . . ." she wasn't sure how far she should tread. "That's kind of horrible."

A trembling expression came over Zoe's face. "Yes, it was. I mean, we'd never even talked about it. He told me he'd had it done when I brought Rachel home."

"Wow," Harper shook her head.

"I don't know why I stayed married to him. Or I guess I do—I loved him. But by the time the marriage was really over, I was too old to have more children." Zoe looked down at Anna, and Harper wondered about that other husband, why he'd deprive Zoe, who was so obviously good at taking care of people, of the chance to have more children.

"I'm sorry," Harper said.

"Well, it was my own foolishness. I should have left him earlier, but I didn't want Rachel to grow up without a father." Zoe looked at her directly. "We're all just figuring it out as we go, you know."

•

THAT NIGHT, HARPER lay in bed thinking about Zoe. It was hard to imagine her married to someone else. Harper wasn't glad it had happened, but in the strange chain of events that could never be calculated, she knew that Zoe's first husband had unintentionally done countless children a favor. Zoe had spent her love on her daughter, and then had love left over for the children she tutored, for her garden, for Harper and Anna.

Life in the country was full of small surprises. A friend of Zoe's brought over an old car seat for Anna. People stopped by for a cold drink or a meal. An Amish farmer delivered some pies as a thank-you for bringing his wife to the hospital. His children had come with him in the carriage, and when they got out, and Harper said "hello," they simply stared.

"They don't speak English," Zoe explained. "They speak German." The girls in black dresses and white aprons, the boys in black pants and wide-brimmed hats, looked like little grown-ups. When Zoe spoke to them in German, they nodded, too shy to speak. Rick talked to the father about picking up some wood at the mill.

After they left, Harper asked, "Does he work at a saw mill?"

"He's got one on his farm," Rick said.

"How do they run a saw mill without electricity?"

"I think they have a generator. They use electricity, but not from the power company. I don't quite understand the rationale, but I figure it's not polite for me to ask. The Amish take trains to visit friends and relatives in Michigan, or they'll pay someone with a flatbed truck to move a woodstove, but they wouldn't drive the truck themselves."

"Sounds complicated."

"Which is ironic when you think about making life simple." Rick tucked up the corner of his mouth, which Harper had learned was his way of smiling.

•

IF SOMEONE HAD described this place to Harper, she would have called it isolated, but even without a television,

Zoe and Rick seemed to know what was going on in the world. They had internet; Zoe listened to NPR in the car when they went to town to do errands.   They visited other farms, or friends stopped by for a meal. Socializing had a different rhythm out in the country.

Harper and Zoe sat on the porch one night as Harper nursed Anna. Frogs and crickets trilled in the blueing air.

"Well, they're ordered," Rick said, stepping out to the porch.

"What's that?" Harper asked.

"The next batch of chickens. Chicks really."

"Where do you get them?" Harper asked.

"They come in the mail."

"No way!" Harper said.

"Yes, way!" Rick imitated her tone, and Zoe and Harper laughed.

Holding Anna, Harper felt happy, flushed with laughter. "How far do they come?"

"These come from Decorah, Iowa. They send them out as soon as they hatch, and they get here the next day."

"Chicks in the mail," Harper grinned. "I'm going to think you're kidding until they actually get here."

19

WHEN HARPER FIRST arrived, she was grateful for Rick and Zoe allowing her a brief retreat, but as the days went by, she felt obliged to look forward and come up with a plan. They'd been so nice, and she didn't want them to get sick of her, but setting out on the road again, without a car and with little money, seemed frightening. Zoe brought the subject up herself after dinner one night.

"Harper, we're glad to have you here, and you're not putting us out, but you do need to start thinking about what you want to do. If you want to stay around here, you should finish high school. There's an alternative high school in Viroqua, The Youth Initiative, but you'd have to figure out child care. I can't watch Anna, because I'll be going back to work myself."

"I know." Harper flushed. "I don't want you to think I've been planning to live off you forever, but I turn eighteen in less than two weeks, and after that, my mother can't make me come home. I know that doesn't solve the whole work and money thing, but mainly, I want to make sure my mother doesn't have . . . I don't know . . . any way to get me back."

"Do you think she's worried about you?"

"No."

"Are you sure?"

Rick had finished eating and got up from the table. "I'm going out to the barn. You call me if you need me," he said.

Harper stood up to clear the table. "What my mother's really afraid of is having me live off her. She doesn't want me back. She wants to go to the bar after work, not worry about a kid." Harper flinched, thinking about the apartment. "I bet our apartment is filthy now. I mean, I cleaned because it made it less depressing to live there, but I bet it's a mess."

"What about getting in touch with your father?"

"From what David told me, I'm not sure he'd be much help."

"Do you still think about finding Nate?"

"Yeah, I do, but when I tried, I didn't have much luck."

"What about his friend—what was his name? Paco? It's an unusual name. If you called the bike shops, you'd probably find him, and you could ask him to have Nate call you here."

She set the plates next to the sink. "My brother told me that Nate, well, I didn't tell him exactly who Nate was, but he told me that no one wants to find out he's a dad like this."

"Well, if you reach him, I imagine it will be an awkward phone call. And if you see him again, it'll probably be strained. But maybe you have to consider short-term awkwardness against long-term concerns." Zoe turned on water and squirted soap into the sink. "What if Anna grows up and wants to find him, and he wishes he'd at least known about her? Or if you do contact him, years from now, and he's upset that you didn't try harder? I think you have to be prepared that, if you see each other again, it might not be a romantic kind of meeting—even though it started out that way." Zoe smiled. "But if he's the kind of person you think he is, he probably needs to know."

Harper took the dishes from the drying rack and put them away to make room for the newly washed dishes. She felt a fluttering under her breastbone, a rising excitement.

"It's two hours earlier there, so businesses would still be open," Zoe said. "Let's see what we find."

When they finished with the dishes, they got on the computer and found the names and phone numbers of the bike stores in Olympia. When Harper called the first store, they told her that Paco worked at Karma Cycles. Zoe smiled at the name, then left Harper to make her call. Harper trembled as she dialed the phone.

"Is Paco there?"

"Yeah, hold on. He's just . . ." Something crashed in the background. "He'll be right there." There was the sound of muffled shouting, and Paco, laughing, picked up the phone. She remembered him falling off the stool at Dunkin' Donuts.

"Hi, Paco, you might not remember me, but this is Harper, I met you last summer, in Sandusky, when you and Nate were driving back to Washington."

"Harper! Dunkin' Donuts girl. I remember you! Where are you calling from? Are you here in Washington?"

"No, I'm not. I'm in Wisconsin. I wanted to get in touch with Nate. I got a postcard from him, but I didn't know his last name or how to reach him, and I knew he was living somewhere without a phone."

"Yeah, Nate's working for Americorps. He doesn't have a landline, but I think he's got a cell. I don't have his number here, but I see him around all the time. Is there a number where he can call you?"

Harper gave him Zoe's number. She felt as if her breath was being squeezed out of her chest. As soon as she hung up, Harper felt an unbearable tension, as if Nate might call back any minute.

•

OVER THE NEXT few days, she jumped every time the phone rang. Sometimes, when she was outside, she imagined it ringing and ringing in the house. She'd run inside, heart pounding, then find it was nothing. Two days later, after dinner, Rick came out to the porch to get her.

"Harper?" he said. "The phone's for you."

Harper handed Anna to Zoe, who smiled her encouragement. Taking the cordless phone, she walked into the shadowed living room. The room was cool, and she shivered.

"Hi," Nate said.

"I hope it didn't seem too weird to call Paco, but I didn't know how else to get in touch with you."

"I sent you a bunch of postcards at the Dunkin' Donuts, but I didn't know if they'd get to you."

"One did."

There was silence. Harper had rehearsed a speech, but it was gone now.

"Listen, this is probably the weirdest phone call you'll ever get, but . . ." She took a breath, clutching the phone. "I had a baby."

"Wow, congratulations, I guess. I—" He stopped. There was a long pause, and she imagined comprehension settling over him. The silence seemed to last forever. "You mean that night?"

"Yes."

"Wow. Oh, wow. I'm going to be quiet for a minute. I have to get my head around this."

Harper squeezed the phone. She heard the faint sound of his breathing. In the silence she heard traffic, a car door slam, a motor in the distance.

"All by yourself? Was your mother horrible?"

"Yes, I did, and yeah, she was."

"Is the baby okay? What kind of baby is it?"

"You keep asking two questions at once. She's a little girl.

Her name is Anna. She's just beautiful."

His voice broke. "You know this is a lot to take in . . ." She heard a garbled sound and couldn't tell if it was a cough or a cry. "I didn't think . . . I . . ."

Silence again. She waited.

"Can I ask you a question—I don't mean it to sound this way, but, why did you keep it? I mean, knowing I was gone, all that."

Her stomach tightened. "I don't know. I just didn't want to have the operation."

"Wow."

She held the receiver, listening, and tried to imagine what it would feel like to get such news. She remembered his long hair, the feeling of waking with him.

"Where are you now?"

"I'm staying with some friends in Wisconsin."

"Are you mad at me?"

"No! I mean, it wasn't your fault."

"Wow. I've got stop saying 'wow.' I sound like a jerk." There was quiet again. "This is weird. Since we're on the phone, I feel like I have to keep talking, but I'm just trying to get my head around this, and I can't talk and think at the same time." He was quiet, breathing into the phone. She thought of him looking down at a box of carefully folded swans. "Listen, I'm actually at work. I just got your message from Paco, and wanted to call, but I have to think for a little while. Can I call you back later on?"

•

WHEN THE PHONE rang late that afternoon, Harper ran for it, but it was the post office calling to say the chicks were in. Rick put on his hat and went out. He returned an hour later with a box of peeping chicks. Anna was mesmerized by the sound.

"You want to help me take them out?" Rick asked.

Harper followed him into the barn.

Zoe came out with them, and held Anna while Harper helped. In a corner, Rick had fashioned a little cardboard corral and filled it with shredded newspaper for bedding, metal waterers, and food.

"They need to have their beaks dipped in water so they know where the water is. All you have to do is pick up a chick, dunk its beak in the pan of water, and they'll figure it out from there."

When he opened the box, Harper couldn't help smiling. Tiny, fluffy little chicks, all in different colors, crowded against one another.

"How do they survive in there?"

"Almost as soon as they're hatched, they're put in the box. I guess they don't need too much food in the beginning."

Harper reached into the box and gently closed her hand around a chick. It chirped loudly, its heartbeat pulsing under her fingers. She lifted it down and dunked its beak in the water. The chick shook itself, and she let it go.

"That's fine," Rick said. "Just like that."

Some of the chicks were butterscotch-colored, some had little dark stripes on their wings. There were fluffy yellow ones, too. Harper picked a russet-colored chick and dunked his beak. "This is amazing! I can't believe they survived in a box."

Once they were in their little corral, a few of the chicks plopped down, sticking a leg out behind them.

"Are they okay?" Harper asked.

"They're fine. Like little kids, they run around then kind of konk out."

"It doesn't look very comfortable."

"Chicken yoga," Rick said.

•

HARPER FOLDED LAUNDRY, bathed Anna, washed jars that Zoe would use for canning. She could tell, precisely because they didn't say it, that Rick and Zoe wondered whether Nate would call back.

When the phone rang after 9:30, Harper felt as if a fire alarm had gone off. She reached for the phone.

"Hi, it's Nate."

She giggled.

"What's so funny?"

"It's not funny." She bit the side of her finger. "It's just that, I'm kind of hiding here because I ran away, which is really another story. My mother lied to Social Services; she tried to get Anna taken away from me, so I had to leave."

"I still don't get . . ."

"Well, no one knows I'm here, so when you said, 'It's Nate,' I laughed because no one else would call me here."

"Oh."

In the silence, fear welled up in her. They didn't connect. This was going to be too hard.

"You want to know something weird?" Harper asked.

"What's that?"

"She has a toenail that's like yours."

"No!"

"She does. Her right toe."

"That's wild." He took a deep breath. "Your mother really tried to have her taken away?"

"Well, she wanted me to give her up for adoption. The thing is, legally, I couldn't give her up without you—you know, the father, signing off." Harper didn't want to talk about legal things, but mentioning the law made the situation seem more real, as if even the outside world presumed some connection between them. She dropped her voice to a whisper. "I didn't know your last name, and it seemed so weird not to know it. I just, I couldn't tell anyone I didn't know it because it seemed like we were just stupid, or that you . . ." She was afraid now, unsure about whether he had felt the same way, or it was just her own imagining. "I just felt really stupid." Harper felt a sob rising in her throat.

"Marcus," Nate said. "Nathaniel Marcus. I didn't know your name either."

"Canaday. Harper Canaday."

"Okay, Harper Canaday."

"It's better now," Harper said. "These people I'm staying with are the nicest people in the world—but I can't just stay here forever, you know?" She wanted to tell him about Zoe rescuing her, about all the things Zoe knew, how she missed her daughter, how nice Rick had been, how she didn't want them to get sick of her.

"Well, I'm working for Americorps now, and I've got a contract. It doesn't pay much, but it's not the kind of thing I can just quit. Do you think you could come out to Olympia?"

"Sure." Her voice sounded tight, uncompliant, but it wasn't how she felt. "You don't have a car, do you?"

"No."

"Do you have any way to get here?"

"Well, I did. That's another story. I've got about $300, but I'm not sure if that's enough for a bus or a train for both of us."

"I'm not sure how I could do this, but do you want me to come and get you?"

"Would you do that?" Harper's voice was hesitant.

"Yeah, I would. I have to arrange it, though. I mean, I'm scheduled this week, but I could say. . . . Well, I'll figure it out. I guess you should give me directions to where you're staying so I can find you."

"Okay. I'm going to give you to Rick. He can tell you how to get here."

"I'll call you when I'm leaving Olympia. Paco and I got back pretty quickly when we drove, so I bet I can make good time."

"That would be great," Harper said.

"Bye for now," Nate said.

And Harper carried the phone outside to Rick, so he could tell Nate how to find them.

20

AT NIGHT, BEFORE sleep, Harper was afraid that Nate wouldn't actually come. What if he never called? Never arrived? It would be a coward's way of saying he just couldn't do it. She remembered his kisses, how they tasted like clean water.

Over the next few days, Harper and Anna spent a lot of time watching the chicks. One would grab a piece of brightly colored newspaper in its beak, run with it, and another chick would chase it, but almost immediately the chicks seemed to forget what they were running after, so they'd pick up a different scrap of paper and start running with that.

"They're so funny." Harper held Anna up so she could see.

"Chicken rugby." Rick grinned.

•

WHEN NATE'S BLUE truck pulled into the driveway, Harper was outside playing with Anna in the grass. She looked up as the truck crunched onto the gravel, the door slammed. When Nate got out, he was a stranger. He was taller than she remembered, and he'd shaved; she could see his face, tan and lean, his lips full. Sun glinted off his glasses. He smiled, and she walked toward him with Anna in her arms.

"Hi," she said.

"Hi." He looked at her, and Harper wondered if she seemed unfamiliar to him as well. He looked down at Anna. "She's so little."

"She's nine weeks old."

He touched Anna's forehead with one finger, ran it along the side of her cheek. "I don't know anything about babies."

The air shimmered around them. Harper felt suddenly older, more grown-up, holding Anna in her arms.

They sat down together in the grass. Nate studied Anna as if he'd never seen a real baby before. Harper set Anna on a blanket, and she waved her arms and legs in the air.

"Are you sure you're not mad at me?"

"Why would I be mad?"

He gave her a long look, as if he wasn't sure he understood her. His brown eyes seemed clear. She wished she could read the future there.

"Neither of us meant for it to happen," Harper said.

"I should have checked in. About the rubber, I mean. I just didn't think it could really happen like that. Or I knew it could happen. I just didn't think it would." He looked off, across the road. "This is a really nice place. How did you get here?"

"It's kind of a long story. Do you want to hold her?" He leaned back a little. "I don't know how."

"Put out your arms."

He stretched forward, held out his arms, and she settled Anna into them. "Just hold her next to you," Harper said.

"She's so tiny," Nate said. "It's hard to believe she's mine." Harper gave him a quick look.

"I don't mean like that."

"Look at her toe." Harper pulled back the blanket to reveal her tiny foot.

He reached down and touched her small toe. "Oh God, that's amazing."

"Or not," Harper smiled.

•

RICK CAME HOME for lunch and busied himself around the barn, looking in on the chicks, changing their water and bedding. He usually did chores in the evening, and Harper could tell he was looking Nate over. Zoe made home-made pizzas for lunch, with tomatoes and basil from the garden. They all sat at the kitchen table, eating pizza, passing Anna between them as they took turns eating.

"So Nate, what kind of projects are you doing for Americorps?" Zoe asked.

"One of the things we're working on is non-native plants that are taking over habitats they weren't intended for. The climate out there is incredible. Coming from the Midwest, it seems like a jungle. Some things, like crown vetch, are good for holding soil in place, but they choke out everything else."

"And Harper said you're living in a yurt?" Rick smiled.

Nate ducked his head, abashed, then reached for another piece of pizza. "It was kind of an experiment. A friend of mine built this place, and he used to live there, but then he met his girlfriend, now she's his wife, and she said the yurt was a no go." He glanced over at Harper. "It was okay for one winter, but I don't know that I'd do it again."

•

AFTER LUNCH, HE and Harper went out to the front yard while Anna napped in the house. They sat down together in the grass.

"I thought about you a lot," Nate said. "But when you think about someone, and you don't see them, it gets pretty big in your mind."

She wanted to say something about how he didn't have to

promise her anything, how they didn't have to pretend, but the words stopped up inside her; she wasn't sure they were true.

They sat and looked out together, across the spreading lawn, past the road to the field and the line of trees beyond.

"So you're sure you want to go back to Olympia with me?"

She thought: what choice do I have? But she did want to go. She nodded.

"You need a place to live with running water. I was thinking about that on the drive. The Americorps stuff doesn't pay much, but we can find an apartment in town. I can always work part-time at the bike shop."

His phrasing ticked in her mind: you, we. They couldn't afford two places, but it would be strange to just move in together. Still, what else could they do?

"Won't your friends think it's weird that you come back with a baby?"

"Well, I told Paco. He'll probably tell our friends."

"This is a crazy way to do anything," Harper said.

"I know. But people do all kinds of things for good reasons, and they turn out screwed up or they don't work out." He scratched at what looked like poison ivy on his arm. "It's still kind of hard to take in. I kept thinking as I was driving: I have daughter. It doesn't make sense. I mean, it feels so random." He looked at Harper, then flushed. "I don't mean it like that. You're not random, but you know what I mean? The thing is, I have this friend, Melissa, whose dad took off, and she's all screwed up about it." He stopped, and Harper wondered who Melissa was, if he meant an old girlfriend. He looked away. "I don't feel like a father, but I mean, she's here, she's alive. If I blew you all off, I'd be somebody's asshole dad. The idea of that seems pretty harsh." He pulled at a blade of grass.

"When I decided to keep her, at first, it wasn't because I wanted to keep her, but because I didn't want to give her away.

I just couldn't imagine giving her to someone else. People kept telling me to do it so it could be like it never happened, but I knew it would never be like that, and I thought—what if I ran into you in the future, years from now, and I told you that we'd had a baby and I gave it away? How weird would that be?"

Nate pushed his hair back behind his ear. "It would be strange. I mean, even if we were both with other people, and we were happy, and had kids and all, it would be like some whole other way that life could have gone."

They sat, side by side, in the grass.

"I should rearrange some things in the back of the truck." Nate stood up and wiped his hands on his jeans.

Harper walked back up to the garden where Zoe was thinning a line of carrots. She sat back on her heels, holding her hand over her eyes against the sun.

"I've never even had a real boyfriend," Harper said. "I feel like I skipped a whole step."

"Do you want to go with him?"

"Yes, but neither of us knows what we're doing."

"Welcome to the planet. You'll sort yourselves out." Zoe took her hand from her forehead; her eyes were green in the sunlight. "I like him. And on a practical level, Anna will have a father, so you'll have some help. I don't mean that in a crass way. She'll get attached to him, you know." Zoe held her gaze. "If I didn't like him, I'd tell you to stay here, but Harper, if it doesn't work out, you call us. We'll help you figure something out."

"You really mean that?"

Zoe stood up and came around to the outside of the fence. She put a dirty arm around Harper's shoulder, then turned and hugged her hard. "Yes, I do."

Harper let herself be hugged, her face in Zoe's warm neck; she was afraid she'd break down and sob.

They walked down to the yard together. Nate crawled out

of the back of the truck. "You ready to go?" Nate called.

"I want to give you the car seat we've been using," Zoe said.

"Are you sure that's okay?" Harper asked.

"It's fine. Carla doesn't want it back."

"I'd like to feed Anna first, get her full."

Harper went into the house to get Anna, who had woken up and started to cry. She changed her and carried her outside. Nate sat down next to her, straightened his legs, bouncing them in the grass. He smelled like peppermint. She lifted Anna to her breast. It might not be perfect, but it would be better than it had been. Nate watched Anna nursing.

"Is that the only food she has now?"

"It's all she needs."

"Pretty amazing."

"Yeah, it is." She brushed a bug off Anna's head. "When they told me it would seem like I was nursing her all the time, I thought they were kidding, but they weren't. In the beginning it was hard, but I'm used to it now. If I hadn't been nursing her in the time I got away from my mother's, she wouldn't have lived. There was no time for bottles, formula, anything like that."

Zoe was in the kitchen, packing food for the trip. When Anna was done, and they went inside, Nate gazed at the food Zoe had gathered: sandwiches, leftover pizzas, fruit and peppers and carrots. She'd packed a styrofoam cooler as well.

"Someone sent me something in this cooler. I don't need it back. I made a bunch of hard-boiled eggs. It'll keep them cold."

"This is an amazing amount of food," Nate said. "We really appreciate it."

"I'm happy to do it," Zoe said, wiping her hands on a dish-towel. "Harper needs to eat well."

Rick had packed up the bassinet. He slid it into the back of the truck and helped Nate get the food in as well.

When it came time to leave, Harper handed Anna to Nate.

She hugged Rick first, who pounded her on the back as if she were choking. Then she hugged Zoe, who smelled of patchouli and garden dirt and basil.

"Thank you so much for everything," Harper said. "I don't know what I . . ." But she started to cry.

"Nothing's over." Zoe smiled. "You'll stop to see us when you come back to visit Nate's family. We want to see Anna in all her little phases." She brushed the hair from Harper's face.

Rick shook Nate's hand. "You give us a call when you get back to Olympia. Let us know you got home safe," Rick said.

They got Anna into her car seat, piled into the truck, and positioned Zoe's food so they could reach it through the small window in the back of the cab.

Nate started the truck and put it into gear.

"I've never met anyone so nice." Harper waved at them through her tears.

Rick and Zoe waved back. Zoe smiled, then her face crumpled, trying not to cry. Harper remembered the day she described her daughter leaving for school and waved again. When Nate started down the gravel driveway, Harper wanted to stop, jump out and run back. The truck swayed from side to side.

"You'll like where we're going," Nate said. "I wanted you to come out a year ago, remember?"

"I never would have thought this," Harper said, wiping her cheek with her hand.

"Me either."

She glanced down at Anna, then to the back of the truck, to make sure they had everything. They would sleep there again, with Anna between them. Harper felt it now, that everything was beginning.

At the end of the driveway, Nate stopped to look both ways: he glanced down at Anna, then turned to Harper.

"Here we go," he said.

ACKNOWLEDGMENTS

Many thanks to Ryan Lynch for his astute comments on an early draft of this novel and to Jen Carlson for reading later on. Barb Nascak, your encouragement will always be remembered. My gratitude to Brent Spencer and Jonis Agee for bringing this book into the world. And to Chad, of course, as this book was dreamed up, while listening to Neil Young, on one of our many road trips.

ABOUT THE AUTHOR

Elizabeth Oness's poems and stories have appeared in *The Hudson Review, Glimmer Train, The Georgia Review, The Gettysburg Review*, and other magazines. Her stories have received an O. Henry Prize, a Nelson Algren Award, and the *Crazyhorse* Fiction Prize. Her books include *Articles of Faith*, winner of the 2000 Iowa Short Fiction Prize; *Departures* (Penguin, 2004); *Twelve Rivers of the Body*, winner of the 2007 Gival Press Fiction Award; and a collection of poems, *Fallibility*, which was selected for the 2008 Many Voices prize and published by New Rivers Press. *Leaving Milan* is the 2014 winner of The Brighthorse Prize in the Novel. Oness directs marketing and development for Sutton Hoo Press, a literary fine press, and is a professor of English at Winona State University. She lives with her husband, C. Mikal Oness, on a farm in southeast Minnesota.